Jess's House

...hool

The Courthouse

The Tangled Mass

The Tangled Mass

A Novel

Cyrus D. Hogue, Jr.

Red Leaf Books
an imprint of October Publishing
Wilmington, N.C.

© 2004 by Cyrus D. Hogue, Jr.

First edition 2004

Red Leaf Books
an imprint of October Publishing
PO Box 12710
Wilmington, NC 28405
www.octoberpublishing.net

ISBN: 0-9747374-1-0

Book and Jacket Design by October Publishing

Cover photographs by Laura McLean, Cyrus D. Hogue
Endpaper photos courtesy of The Robert Fales Collection and the Louis T. Moore collection, New Hanover County Public Library, Wilmington, NC

Applied for Library of Congress Cataloging-in-Publication Data.

09 08 07 06 05   04   6 5 4 3 2 1

Printed in Canada.

To: The Superior Court Judges holding Courts in the Fifth Judicial District, and to the officers of those courts who patiently served me during some fifty years of practice.

Down, Down, Down,

Until the depths do cease,

Comes a clearing in the tangled mass

Of Human debris,

Cast along the crumbling walls of time,

The life of toil is through.

And we reach that place,

Of which only Dante knew,

In which that fiend from paradise,

Did make unto the place,

Where sinners go to find

Their roots of happiness, and

In the ultimate end to see

Really how good their lives must be.

CDH 1937

Acknowledgments

I must acknowledge the help that people have given me in preparing this manuscript.

First, Nicole Smith and Nicki Leone of October Publishing, who carefully read the preliminary, formatted it, and made many pertinent corrections and suggestions.

My wife, Mary Ann Hogue, who redid the first part, encouraged me, and kept me going with her love.

Victoria Strachan, who kept my software straight, read a draft, and helped.

John J. Burney, Jr. and his brother Louis, who read it and gave me encouragement.

All the others who read the manuscript and encouraged me to continue, including: my late friend John Baker Saunders; Roi Penton; Jack Eschelman; Kelly Repko; Amy Thompson; and Frances Wood.

Although I did not follow all of their thoughts, I thank them all.

The Tangled Mass

Prologue

J ake Jones, a slightly built, blonde, fifteen year old, twisted in his chair as he listened to the prosecuting attorney interrogate witnesses in the State's case against Degar Loghin, who was on trial for killing his daughter Tess. Jake was summoned as a witness for the prosecution and that morning as his father, Caleb Jones, was driving him to the courthouse he had broken his silence.

"You know Dad, I'm not 100 percent sure, but I think Mr. Loghin may be guilty of killing Tess."

"Well now son, don't have any preconceived ideas like that. When they ask you a question, you answer it as truthfully as you can."

"Oh I'll do that, but she told me time and time again how mean he was to her. He even beat her with his belt and slapped her lots of times and—"

"Well son, that certainly was no way for Mr. Loghin to treat Tess, whatever she had done, but that doesn't mean he would kill her. You know what she told you, if not in his presence, would be hearsay and not allowed in evidence"

"I know that, but did I tell you that she was in the hospital on Thanksgiving night? They let her go home, but to get sick again so soon . . . well I just think he's guilty. Tess was such a sweet girl, not the prettiest one I knew, but she did have pretty red hair. Her life wasn't easy. I really felt sorry for her lots of times . . . I just hope she had some happy times."

"I'm sure she did You two certainly seemed to hit it off well."

"Yeah, I guess we did. I have to admit I really have missed her. She was kind and she was smart . . . always on the honor roll. I would have liked to go to her funeral but she was buried even before I knew she was dead!"

Caleb turned to Jake as they approached the courthouse.

"All right Jake we're nearly there. Just remember to answer the questions. Don't tell them what you think. Tell them what you know happened. Oh . . . and don't be nervous. Just tell them the truth and you'll be a good witness. I'll stop and let you out and then I'll come up to the trial. You know where to go, don't you?"

"Yes"

After Jake had entered the courtroom, he thought back to the time he first really remembered Tess: It was the first day that they both started to school.

Part I

1928-1936

Chapter One

The old brass, iron-clappered school bell rang out clearly on a crisp morning in September, 1928. Mrs. Cling, the principal at the Sunset Park School, had been swinging the bell for many years; its handle was worn. The school was a rather small building located on Beach Road south of Wilmington, North Carolina. As the bell sounded, the snail-paced boys on the road started to hasten their steps a bit so as not to be late and suffer the after-school penalty of describing their infraction many times in writing on the blackboard. Most of the first graders were already in their seats anticipating the new venture of learning, and also anticipating the relief of being out from under the watchful eyes of their parents.

Tess Loghin, a thin, redheaded, freckle-faced girl, had been one of the first to arrive, taking her seat on the second row of the first-grade class. As she walked to school that morning many random thoughts had passed through her head. Most of these musings concerned her stepmother and father and the state of their living conditions, which were poor under any criteria. It was hard for her to understand why her father was so cross with her when she tried her best to do the chores he expected her to do around the house. Degar Loghin worked as a mechanic for the Atlantic Coast Line Railroad headquartered in town. He received a small paycheck twice a month, and after a few drinks of bootleg whisky at a nearby bar, he would bring home the remainder. With much ado he would gruffly announce—and usually his words were the same:

"It's time for us to go to the grocery store. Come on. I don't have all day. Damn it to hell! You two can't seem to imagine how much money it costs me to take care of you! In addition to food there are other expenses you know, so don't be whining at me to buy things we don't absolutely need!" Then he would slam out of the house.

Seated a row behind Tess was a small towheaded boy, almost seven years old, who lived in the big house on Central Boulevard about two blocks from the school. He, like Tess, had been born shortly after the September 30 deadline, so he started school older than most of the first-graders in that county. Tess happened to glance up when Jake came in; she remembered seeing him before, usually when she went with her daddy to buy groceries. He never said much, but he would return her "Hi." She noticed, and with a bit of envy, that he always seemed to have a nickel to buy a Baby Ruth; she was lucky to get a penny to buy a Mary Jane. Sometimes his sister was with him; she was a year older and probably in the second grade, and she no doubt had been with him that morning walking to school. One time at the store she heard his mother call him Jake, and later her daddy said that the lawyer who lived in the big house on Central Boulevard

4

was Caleb Jones, Jake's father. Before the class started, Tess turned and took a furtive glance at Jake in the hopes that he might return her look with a smile, but there was no emotion on his face as he waited patiently for his education to start.

Almost filling the doorway, Mrs. Cling came in with a lovely, young brunette woman, maybe around twenty-five years old.

"Good morning children. I'm Mrs. Cling, your principal here at Sunset Park. This is Miss Bradley. She's your teacher for first grade this year. You must pay close attention to her instructions and be obedient to her requests. It's of utmost importance since you are here to attain an education."

With this she bustled out the door. Miss Bradley looked around the room at the eager students and smiled. "Welcome each and every one of you. I'm so happy to be here, and just seeing your smiling faces, you must be happy too. The first thing we need to do is to introduce ourselves, maybe even say what you like to do, that way we'll learn a little about each other. Now I'm Miss Bradley, as Miss Cling said, and my most favorite thing to do is teach school," she said.

After each child followed her example she asked Jake and another boy to pass out the first-grade reader, which was a story about Baby Rae with applications of the alphabet on every page.

So the first grade of school began for Tess and Jake. The simple scene it presented showed little indication of the complicated and tragic circumstances that would surround them in the future.

As they finished their first day and were leaving school, Jake heard one of the boys teasing Tess. "Red-headed gingerbread! Ain't worth a cabbage head!" Tess apparently didn't hear it, or pretended not to hear it. It made Jake really uncomfortable; he had never heard anyone speak so tauntingly to another person.

But Tess, as she walked down the road for home, was as happy as she had ever been. She had a book to take home and it had pictures in it of all sorts of things, with the spelling of the words shown below. That day she learned many new words. Miss Bradley had been especially nice to her and had encouraged her when she stumbled over one of the sentences. As she came to the big house on Central Boulevard she turned to Jake, who was walking slightly behind her.

"Isn't that the house you live in?"

"Yes, I live there with my mother, father, and my sister Jane, and we have a dog named Wiggles. You must come to see us sometime. Hey, do you see that big chinaberry tree over near the wall? Well, I climb it all the time, and some day I hope to put a tree house in it."

"Really? I've never seen a tree house but I've heard of them. Maybe after you build it I can come over and see it. I've never climbed a chinaberry tree and I've never been in a tree house. I'd like to know what one is like. I hope you'll tell me when it's ready."

"Sure I'll be glad to do that." Jake replied, smiling at her.

Tess thought Jake was friendly and pleasing, and she remembered how he was the only one who didn't laugh at her when she made a mistake that morning, so she smiled back at him. Those happy thoughts and cheer were soon interrupted by the dread of going home. Her mother had died some years ago, not long after Tess was born. Life had not been kind to Tess in several ways, and when she turned six her father made her do a lot of the house cleaning even though she had a stepmother. When he was leaving for work yesterday he had told her to clean the bathroom, which she did. But after he took a bath and washed off the grease from the roundhouse it was dirty again.

"Tess, I told you to clean the bathroom and it looks a mess!" he yelled. When she told him she had cleaned it, he slapped her. "Don't you sass me! You evidently didn't do a good job the first time so clean it again."

At times like these she wished for her mother. Tess was too young to remember when or how her mother had died, but she knew that if she were still here things would be different. In church they had told her to pray, and each day she prayed that her mother could somehow return and take care of her. She only had a few memories of her grandmother and grandfather, Mary and Bailey Mann, who lived in South Carolina. She lived with them way back, right after her mother died. When Tess returned to Wilmington her father would occasionally take her back to visit them. These days he said he was too busy. The Mann's didn't have an automobile so they weren't able to come and see her. Once she had talked to them long distance on the phone and she remembered how happy she felt when they told her they loved her.

Tess arrived home, a small, wooden, two-bedroom house, which was certainly a much less opulent setting than some of the houses closer to the school. A big, scroungy-looking hound dog with a dismal expression on its face and a hungry look met her at the edge of the yard with a tail-wagging welcome.

"Hello Sis," she said as she patted the dog. "You're such a good dog. Look I have a book, see? I've been to school!"

Her stepmother, Ginny, was in the house reading a movie magazine and didn't even look up at Tess as she went to the kitchen for something to eat.

On Jake's short walk home, past the small grocery store and Cannon's filling station, he was filled with thoughts of reading. His mother had given him a love for books by reading him Bible stories and books about Robin Hood, Tom Sawyer, and other exciting childhood characters, but now he was looking forward to reading those books himself.

After Tess went on her way he walked under the chinaberry tree, which not only shaded the edge of the yard, but was also a fun tree to climb; it also provided green ammunition for his slingshot at times. As he climbed the retaining wall at the edge of the yard he thought of Tess. He didn't understand why she seemed so sad when all the other girls seemed happy. When they played during recess Tess didn't join in.

No one was home at Jake's house but Carrie the maid and Wiggles the fox terrier. Wiggles jumped on him at the front door to welcome Jake home.

"Carrie, I'm home! I'm home!" He smelled the aroma of Carrie's baking as he dashed into the kitchen.

"Well now honey, tell me. How was your fuss day at school?" she asked, enfolding him in her voluminous arms.

"Oh it was wonderful, just wonderful. I have a book and I'm gonna go upstairs to my room and read it."

"Now you jist wait a minute! Your Momma wanted you to have some cookies and a glass of milk when you got home. You can take it all upstairs with you to enjoy while you look at your book."

He climbed the stairs with cookies in his pocket and the milk and book in his hands. Inside his large bedroom he closed the door, stretched out on the bed, and savored his precious book, forgetting the milk and cookies on the table. Wiggles, though forbidden upstairs, followed and cuddled up beside him on the bed.

After enjoying his book for a while, turning each page one by one, noticing repetitions of words and trying to guess what some of them were from the pictures, Jake ran down the steps two at a time with Wiggles close at his heels. "I'll be back soon," he shouted to Carrie. They ran out the door and across the road to the heavily-wooded acreage. At the other end of Central Boulevard was the river, about a mile wide at that point. His daddy had driven him down that way now and then, and Jake thought if he could learn to swim he might be able to swim across the river—or better still, make a sailboat and sail down to the Atlantic Ocean about twenty miles away.

Jake and Wiggles entered the beautiful woodlands, covered mostly with scrub oaks that had already begun to turn orange. There was a slight hint of fall in the air. Someone had told him that there was a lake on the other side of the wooded area, but had warned him not to go near it because of the snakes and alligators. He and Wiggles roamed the woods for a while, something they loved to do. Jake was fond of the outdoors and dreamed that maybe he would be able to work at some outdoor job when he grew up. After a while they returned home and Jake joined his family for dinner.

The Joneses home had been built in the more opulent times of the twenties and contained a large entrance hall. A wide stair descended from a large balcony with beautifully turned balusters; a skylight provided central lighting for the stairway and front hall during the day. The living room and study were gracious rooms highlighted by large fluted columns and trimmed out with handsome moldings. The rest of the house was equally as pleasing to the eye. It had been built by one of the developers in the area—an area that had once held promise—but the development had not been successful. Jake's father purchased the house at a distress sale in 1924. Their home, located on Central Boulevard, was a fine and prosperous looking house but expensive to maintain. Caleb was a well-educated and articulate lawyer with loyal clients in town, but during the Great Depression only a few had money to pay him for his services. The beautiful house that had once given Caleb a sense of accomplishment proved burdensome as time passed.

Chapter Two

The following day Degar Loghin was in a terrible mood when he left home for his job at the Coastline, a mood that matched the rather dark and dreary day. He knew that he was scheduled to work on the airbrake system of Engine 544, an engine that always seemed to have something wrong with it. One reason for his ill mood was that Ginny refused to come to him the night before. To add to all that she and Tess were slow getting his grits and sausage on the table for breakfast this morning. He resented the fact that Tess had started school; now it would take her away from home and prevent her from helping with the chores. Besides, he didn't like the idea of her associating with some of the kids in that school.

Degar was a fairly tall man with dark features that seemed even darker from the years he'd spent working in a hot greasy area. Aside from this, he was not bad looking, and when dressed up he had a debonair look about him. His given name was Degar, but he had no idea where the name had come from. Years ago his mother had offered a possible clue.

"Can't imagine why your pa named you Degar. For the life of me, the only thing I can think of is that it rhymes with 'cigar.' Seems your granddaddy always had one in his mouth and your father thought the world of his papa. Maybe he believed it was a way to name you for him," she'd said.

Degar stormed out of the small wooden house on Beach Road. He got into his black, second-hand Model-T Ford, purchased recently for thirty-five dollars. The truck's bands didn't catch immediately when he stepped on the gas pedal and this hyped his mood even more. Finally getting the car started, he drove north on Beach Road past the small school and the dam known as Brown's Lake. Nearing downtown, he passed through the area called Dry Pond and eventually came to several blocks of very large homes. This was an area sometimes known as Pigeon Hill, where the most affluent of the community lived. It was so known because pigeons would roost on the slate of these handsome, often mansard-roofed houses. He passed the two large churches, Presbyterian and Episcopalian, both built close to the sidewalk and overlooking Third Street. He continued on past the red brick courthouse, which was the second largest building in town, and by the white city hall with its large hand-some columns. Farther down the street he turned left and, crossing the railroad tracks, he arrived at the roundhouse and shops of the Atlantic Coast Line Railroad.

Atlantic Coast Line was created by a combination of the Wilmington and Weldon Railroad and the Wilmington, Florence and Augusta, both of which provided freight and passenger services for the small port city. There was still another railroad, at one time called the Wilmington, Brunswick and Southern, which ran about twenty-five miles south to Southport. In the heyday of the WB&S the rather robust president received passes on other railroads, and, when questioned about the WB&S being a truly authentic railroad he was always heard to say, "It might not be as long as some railroads but it's just as wide."

The roundhouse was behind the passenger station concourse. The concourse was in a cut, which made it easy to back trains into the station. With the train so close to the entrance the passengers didn't have long walks to and from the trains. The "roundhouse" was a large semi-circular building with sixteen bays, a maze of tracks and switches which allowed several locomotives to enter at one time. There was a large turntable in front that enabled the mechanics to turn the engines around for their entrance into the bay and for their exit to the main tracks after the work was done. Under some of the tracks there were pits in which workers could descend in order to work on the under carriage. There were about twenty workers, both black and white, on each nine-hour shift.

Degar had a locker where he kept his personal tools, his coveralls, and his gloves.

He put these on each morning of the six-and-a-half-day workweek. He arranged himself after putting on his work clothes and reported to Bob Callus, the foreman on his shift.

"Degar, Engine 544 came in with the morning train from Washington, but it was a little late so it's just now being shifted to the roundhouse. For the time being I'd like you to join a cleanup group that's 'tempting to remove the grease from the roundhouse floors," Bob said.

Degar liked Callus. Bob was a good man and a dependable

foreman, but Degar still didn't like doing such a menial job. After he got a mop Degar halfheartedly joined the group and began to help. Only about fifteen minutes had passed when Engine 544 came puffing into the roundhouse at a very slow speed. It was switched to Bay 5 above a four-foot-deep pit that barely cleared the engine's undercarriage.

"Degar, the engineer reported that 'ole 544 isn't braking properly and he thought there might be a leak in the reserve air tank. How about you getting under it now to see what you can find out? I'll get into the cab and make sure the compressor is working properly," Callus called out.

Working in the pit was a difficult and dirty job and Degar hated it. The pit was not only just four feet deep but also only four feet wide and it was full of the residue of a mixture of coal dust, cinders, and grease. Degar reluctantly descended into this depository amidst small jets of steam that whistled around him. As he moved around some of the spurts brushed his coveralls. Being a tall man, he had to duck in order to get completely beneath the undercarriage of Engine 544.

"Okay, my psi reading is good. How about the gauge in the cab?" Degar called up after he had attached a gauge to the reserve tank relief valve. With further investigation he discovered a leak on the line from the tank to the cylinder that activated the brake shoe on the right drive wheel. Degar stopped the leak and tightened all the fittings.

"Hey Callus, increase the pressure. I'll see if there are any other leaks." When he found no additional leaks he started out of the pit.

"Hey, wait a minute Degar," called Callus. "While you're

14

under there, how about checking all of the other air brake fittings?"

Degar grudgingly went back down. The entire directive took about six hours of the day and when Degar emerged with a sore back, he was saturated with sweat and black railroad grease. While he had been working on old 544, he thought of how a foreman like Callus didn't get hot and greasy every day. Callus also got to travel on the line from time to time to supervise repairs in other cities. Sometimes he had to go as far away as Chicago and New York City, and Degar had heard him speak of some of the delights available on such trips. When he wasn't grousing about his job, Degar fretted about his hard life and how the cost of feeding Tess and Ginny seem to be increasing daily.

After finishing up the job he stumbled out of the pit, changed out of his dirty, greasy coveralls, washed up a bit, and left the shops at about half past four. He went immediately to the North Side Bar 'N Grill. Even though prohibition was in effect you could still enjoy a steady supply of white moonshine spirits at a cost of ten cents a shot. Several other tired shop workers and men from the railroad office building were at the bar. One of the latter was his best friend, Jere Swain. Jere worked in the Freight Traffic department; he was a white-collar worker and made more money than Degar, but it didn't interfere with their friendship. He and Jere had both been employed by the railroad about four years back, and their common talk was usually about the low pay and the long hours. They also talked about fishing, which Jere enjoyed and Degar hoped to some day. After they downed a couple of drinks Degar drove home. As he went along his bad mood, which had been eased somewhat with the moonshine, returned. He continued to think about the misfortunes in his life—hard work, his low pay, and the cost of keeping up a family. There didn't seem to be any good answer to his miserable life; it was just another awful day added to a long line of awful days.

When he parked in the yard, his hound dog Sis trotted over and tried to welcome him home. She received a firm kick in return for her affection. His mood followed him into the house.

"When's my supper going to be ready Ginny? Why is Tess in the bathroom? She's always in there when I get home from work. Hurry up in there, I need to take my bath!" he yelled, banging on the door. Shortly Tess emerged.

"Sorry Papa."

"Ginny I want my supper as soon as I get out!"

"Don't worry Degar, supper is ready," Ginny sighed.

"Well I don't want any cold food. You keep it hot!"

After supper Degar rolled into bed and called out to Ginny. "Soon as you and Tess wash up the dishes you come on in here, and make it fast."

After Ginny joined Degar in the bedroom Tess could hear their noisy talk and the ultimate quiet of their love-making. She lay in her bed thinking of her dead mother, hungering for her love, and praying one more futile time for her return.

Degar had married his first wife, Grace Mann, in 1918. Grace grew up in South Carolina and met Degar when he was a World War I recruit in a camp near her home. They had a swift courtship and were married just before he was sent overseas near the end of the war. He never made combat, and returned home after swinging through the French countryside, accepting the many embraces and gifts from the French girls and celebrating the victory that he had done very little to bring about. His appetite for women was enhanced by these encounters and when he returned to Grace he found that his feelings for her had diminished. He continued to look around. Grace became pregnant after his return. Tess was born in 1921, a scrawny little red-headed baby girl that her mother nursed and loved with all her heart. Grace was sickly after Tess' birth, and about a year later had a bout with what was called acute indigestion. The doctor prescribed pills, but she continued to suffer acute pain and died in 1922 in great misery of purported heart failure. Tess' grandparents came up near the end, and on her deathbed Grace said she thought she had been poisoned. "It must have been food poisoning," Degar had said. Grace was transported to South Carolina for burial and Degar and Tess accompanied the casket.

When the funeral was over, Degar confronted Grace's parents.

"We need to talk about Tess. I'm sorry, but there's no way I can take care of her! I have to work and there's no woman in the house to see to her. When I get back to Wilmington I'm taking her to a foster home so she can be placed up for adoption."

"Oh no Degar, please don't do that. We can take care of Tess. We can afford to do it and we love her," replied Mary.

"I don't know about that . . . she'll be here in South Carolina and I'll be in Wilmington. If something happened to y'all where would I be then?"

"But Degar, let us take care of her 'til you've at least gotten over Grace's death—maybe even remarried. You can come and see her any time you want, and we promise to take good care of little Tess until you can do it."

The Manns were finally successful and Degar accepted their suggestion: Tess would remain with her grandparents until Degar recovered from his grief and was able to provide for her. When he returned to Wilmington Degar collected the small insurance policy he had on Grace, a policy he had acquired by paying a dollar a week.

Tess stayed in South Carolina until Degar married his second wife, Ginny. Her grandparents grew to love her very much, and she them, and they were heartbroken when the time came for little Tess to go to Wilmington with Degar a year or so later. It was sad because they seldom saw Tess after that.

At the time Grace died, Ginny was working as a waitress in a café near the railroad station and Degar had had his eye on her for a long time—even before Grace died. Ginny had heard that Degar's wife died a very painful death, and there was even some talk that she had been poisoned. But at the time she was glad to find a man who had a steady job with the railroad, and it was a lot better than what she had known on the farm in South Carolina as one of seven children. When she came to Wilmington, she had little knowledge of the more worldly confrontations she would have in a larger town. She had been married before to her high school sweetheart, which resulted in a little dance around until he ran off with another girl, leaving her broke and unhappy. The divorce had become final about a month before she left home.

Ginny married Degar in 1922 after a sporadic courtship consisting mostly of trips to the South Beach with his friends where they enjoyed dancing and swimming. After the marriage, Degar brought Tess, barely more than a baby, back from her grandparents' to live with them, and in a way Ginny had grown to love the child as her own. Degar told her that he didn't want to have other children. He had too much experience with a baby after his first wife's death, and the cost and trouble of tending to them was more than he ever wanted again.

Tess clung to Ginny as if she were her mother, for she was much too young to remember her real mother. As she grew older she learned about Grace Mann, and they all prayed for her soul in heaven. At times, the Loghins went to the Baptist church nearby, and when Tess was five she went to Sunday school to learn about the baby Jesus. Over time, Degar seemed to resent his daughter more and more. He was forever nagging her about her looks and expected her to do chores, even though she was too young to perform most of what he required.

Although Ginny desired children of her own, she accepted the idea of Tess being her daughter and took over the daily task of tending to her. Degar, though he never really wanted the child, began to show affection for her on occasion. Tess continued to grow in this somewhat dysfunctional household, but when she started attending school, her rather meager life started to blossom a bit. Tess walked to school each morning, except for those occasions when a neighbor would drive by and pick her up; Degar drove right by the school every day on his way to work and had never driven her.

Chapter Three

The Freight Traffic department of the Atlantic Coast Line was in a three-story red brick building that extended nearly two blocks from the passenger terminal to Compress Street. The west side of the building faced the river, from which the prevailing wind came, so it was cooler if you were lucky enough to have your desk there. Across the river, which was about a quarter mile wide, you could see the wet lowlands covered with cypress trees, a fresh green color in the spring that turned to a lovely golden yellow in the fall. Each floor of the building contained a maze of desks occupied by men dressed in shirts and ties, their coats hung over the back of their chairs because of the heat that usually consumed the place. The windows, open most of the time, had glass deflectors to keep the breeze, when it existed, from blowing the many papers all over the room. To the south and to the rear of the river was Compress Warehouse where cotton, which came in by boat, wagon, or train, was pressed into bales of 1000 pounds and prepared for transport by rail or ship to other parts of the world.

When a ship came to be loaded or unloaded, the musical chant of the stevedores could be heard in the Freight Traffic offices, adding some soothing relief to the dreary work being performed there. A deep roaring horn announced the arrival and departure of the ships. This added some diversion for the employees and many would get up to look out the window—possibly wishing they were traveling to some foreign and exotic place.

The railroad headquarters was located downtown, and the general office, from which the president directed the company, was about a block north of the Freight Traffic building. The head office also housed the various vice-presidents, and those who were lucky enough to work there referred to the Freight Traffic office as the zoo. The office was given this name because of the diverse nature of the people who worked there.

The Freight Traffic department was the heart of the railroad. Passenger traffic was declining with the development of the gas-powered automobile, but commercial traffic had really always been the mother lode of railroad business. When freight was loaded on any part of the railroad, the teletype received a copy of the bill of lading with the number and location of the particular freight car involved. From that point forward each car of the railroad carrying freight was tracked according to its origin and destination. The billing department was notified so that the projected revenue could also be recorded. Teletype advised the progress of the car and the ultimate delivery of cargo to its destination and issued a report that the freight costs had been collected or properly billed to a creditworthy customer. Many times a car would be mis-switched, lost, or otherwise mishandled. This would cause much confusion and angry recriminations from the supervisor, who constantly patrolled the aisles making sure that everyone was attending to their work. The whole scenario created voluminous piles of paper, which were all carefully recorded and filed in case there were claims for lost freight or damage.

Cotton had not quite abdicated its throne in the South, and with the boll weevil somewhat subdued and the mechanical picker more prevalent, the supply was steady. Jere Swain worked on the second floor and was in charge of tracking the loading and shipping of cotton bales, some of which were loaded right outside his window. Most of the cotton came out of Memphis or New Orleans, and sometimes Houston, and was transferred from the Louisville and Nashville railroad.

Jere enjoyed his white-collar job with its five-day workweek. It gave him the luxury of being off all day on Saturday unless there was an emergency. A lost car, for example, meant he had to report to work immediately. Jere lived in the eastern part of town near the streetcar line that went to North Beach and downtown. He was able to walk two blocks from his home each morning to board the trolley and arrive for work at eight o'clock.

Jere loved fishing, and he was able to take the streetcar from his home to the Sound to fish for spot and flounder when the season was good. He and his wife lived in a nice house with their two children who attended school nearby, and they were indeed leading a happy—if not too prosperous—life. His pay was meager for a white-collar worker, but twice a month he received pay for his efforts, which was sufficient to keep his family clothed, fed, pay the rent, and provide him an occasional trip to the North Side Bar 'N Grill for a drink with his friend Degar.

On the third floor of the Freight Traffic building a vice president of the railroad, Thomas Cole, had an office with a large desk and leather chairs. Jere had, on one occasion, been there. When a particularly large shipment of cotton had been switched to the wrong line on its way from Memphis to Birmingham Jere had solved the problem. Mr. Cole had been particularly nice to Jere, and called him in to personally thank him. This was about the only time there had been any congeniality in his office life. He knew, as did all of the other workers, that if he dropped dead tomorrow, all the trains would leave on time and there would be no change in the routine of the "zoo."

One day Jere left work at five o'clock and went to the bar to join his friend Degar.

"Well what's up!"

"Just the same 'ole things," replied Degar. "I work my tail off for what? A measly amount of dough that hardly keeps body and soul together. Hey tell me, have you been fishing lately?"

"Sure have. You know, bringing home some fish can help the weekly budget."

"I could use some help there. I can't believe what things cost today! I hope come fall I'll be getting some Saturdays off, but my work schedule is so awful I doubt that I can go floundering with you any time soon—never been either!"

"Maybe some day. Maybe before long."

He and Jere continued to lament their sad state and the bleak future that lay ahead of them. After enjoying his drink and the mostly dismal conversation, Degar left and went to his car.

As Jere walked about three blocks to catch the streetcar he was thinking that some day, after his children were grown, he might be able to buy a car. He could go fishing somewhere other than in the Sound. Mainly he could ride back and forth to work as Degar did. When he got home his wife and two children met him with a warm greeting. He put his arm around his son.

"Guess what son? The Pirates are playing in the ball field at Dawson and Seventeenth Streets on Saturday. We'll have to check it out. Would 'ja like to go?"

"Golly, would I! Dad, I'd love to go."

"Oh, I forgot to tell you. Shooney Jones is going to catch and "Shoeless Joe" Batts is scheduled to pitch. I'll try to get a couple of tickets for us tomorrow." Jere hoped that the boy would become interested in baseball and try to make the high school team in a few years. Maybe he would even play well enough to make an AA team—maybe even the Capitols in Raleigh. Even though Ted was young, the job market future in Wilmington looked mighty bleak. Maybe another area would be more promising. The suggestion for Saturday excited Ted, but at his age he was probably more interested in the hoped-for peanuts and Orange Crush than in the game.

That Saturday at the ball park Jere and Ted ran into Caleb and Jake. It took Caleb some persuasion to talk his son into coming to the game, but once Caleb was successful Jake got excited about it. Caleb and Jere were casual friends; they had met at a game sometime back and they frequently sat together at the ballpark. The boys enjoyed talking to each other as they ate boiled peanuts and drank Orange Crush. Near the end of the game a pop fly came sailing into the stands near Ted and he was able to wrest the ball away from the person next to him. That was the real victory of the game as far as they were concerned. The Pirates were handily defeated by the New Bern Angels. When the boys went home they were tired yet happy, full of the delights of the game—mainly the peanuts and drinks they consumed. Those goodies greatly spoiled their appetites.

Chapter Four

The headquarters building of the railroad housed all of the executive offices. On the fifth and top floor was the opulent office of the president. Adjacent was the office of the financial vice president, who daily pored over the waves of cash flow statements that came in from the various stations and outside offices, mostly the Freight Traffic department. His biggest responsibility was assuring that there was sufficient cash to cover the payroll on the third and eighteenth of each month.

The president was a robust man with many social attributes and a large house on North Beach, where he spent the summers entertaining the many railroad customers who came into the area. In town he lived on "Pigeon Hill" in a large Georgian house with a slate roof. He was active in one of the large churches a block or so away, and was particularly in religious ardor when the annual giving campaign was in progress. A personal steward attended to his needs on his sumptuous private railroad car, which was frequently attached to the end of the train whenever it carried him to destinations from New York to Florida. There was a speedometer installed in his car so that he could monitor the engineer's performance—from whether he passed through towns properly to whether or not he used excessive speed to meet a schedule. The engineers were proud to be hauling him, but they were always aware that any deviation from proper procedure would be called to their attention.

The social life within the upper echelons of railroad employees centered around which families could be closest to the president's circle. Teeming with social lust, the executive's wives worked hard to be included in any activity initiated by his wife. It was important to them to make her aware of the valuable contributions their spouses were providing to the railroad. Of particular interest to these social climbers was a German dance club that held two social events, one at Christmas and Easter respectively. To be excluded was a social disaster.

There was an elevator in the headquarters building, but if an employee was summoned from the first floor he didn't dare take it. Instead he hastily bounded up the stairs to promptly attend to the call; many in the higher echelon were known to pop a nitroglycerin pill when they reached the fifth-floor level out of breath. Heart attacks were a risk of doing business at the railroad.

The Legal department on the fourth floor was staffed by the General Counsel, clerks and secretaries who, with many carbons, turned out the documents to support the litigation in all parts of the line. One of the Legal department's main jobs was to make sure that political support was thrown to judicial candidates who were friendly to the railroads and would rule in their favor. They also stroked legislative candidates who opposed passing laws that would require warning signals and gates at the many grade crossings over the system. Their success in these matters was clearly shown by the many favorable verdicts the railroad had received—and by the many impoverished families, widows, and orphans of those who dared to cross the line on foot or in automobiles.

Heading this department was an attractive lawyer, William David, known as Bill, whose personality eschewed the fact that he was a descendant of a cabinet member of the Confederate States of America. He spent his days furthering the good cause of keeping the railroad popular in each county, town, city, or state in which it had a line. The Davids had a home in the mansion district that was sandwiched between two large, fine houses belonging to kin of an oil baron who had very generously endowed his relatives. Situated between their two handsome, ten-foot walls he jokingly referred to his home as the "The Waldoff." A block over was the home of a prominent lawyer and judge with whom he consulted regularly about the status of the courts and legislature in order to keep up with the winds of time as they pertained to the railroad.

The Legal department was also in charge of all union relations, which mostly consisted of keeping the various departments from unionization. It also lobbied to prevent trucking companies from obtaining routes competitive to the railroad. As the freight rates for traffic out of Norfolk to the north and Charleston to the south were more favorable than those in town, it discouraged the development of the port on the river. There wasn't much opportunity for industry to use this readily available asset, or for the port to develop.

The Executive department had issued a policy to the effect

that the railroad should discourage all new business from moving into town in order to keep control of the labor market. In this way, the railroad could protect itself from losing employees and from wage competition. Their efforts were hugely successful and Wilmington had grown very little, if any, since the end of the Great War in 1918. In fact, when the Coastline started in 1900, Wilmington was the largest city in North Carolina; by 1910, it no longer had that honor. The war had injected a little prosperity into the area in the form of a shipyard that made concrete ships. Except for the railroad payroll and some money from the tobacco crop that trickled into town in the fall, the prosperity of the local merchants was naturally limited.

From the passenger station, a large concourse that adjoined the headquarters building, the trains left north to Washington and New York, and south to Atlanta. They made connections at many points along the line to most of the other railroads on the east coast. Degar Loghin had walked many times through the concourse to assist brakemen with dysfunctional air hose attachments, but had yet to ride a train to an attractive destination.

Access to the town by road from the west stopped at the river, but was supplemented by two ferries. One, named the *John Knox,* plied the short distance daily and landed at the foot of Market Street where the old slave market stood as a grim reminder of days long past.

So it was in this atmosphere that Degar and Jere each carried out his assigned dull, and sometimes burdensome, duties in support of the railroad.

There were two hotels in town, the Orton on the main street, and one bearing the town's name close to the railroad station. It

29

was here that the tradesmen—who continually came to town to sell supplies and equipment to the railroad—stayed, and where the employees who were in charge of purchasing enjoyed the gratuities provided by them. This was particularly true at the Orton Hotel, which maintained a dining room famous for its cuisine, particularly delicious in the fall when it served quail and duck. At times they even served the small ricebirds (soon to be extinct) that fed in the fields west of the river and were harvested brutally with sticks by lantern at night.

Chapter Five

In the late 1920s and early 1930s there were many changes throughout the country. One such change was the election of Franklin Roosevelt, a democrat, as the president of the United States.

In 1933 Caleb Jones was enchanted by the election of Roosevelt and his promise to eliminate fear and, through his various administrative creations such as the CCC, NRA, CWA, and WPA, to provide jobs for the unemployed and return the country to prosperity. A strong democrat, Caleb was very close to the congressman of his district, and through him was able to acquire two seats in the House of Representatives for Roosevelt's opening address to Congress. Jake accompanied his father on this trip and was impressed by being in the House Chamber balcony, seeing all the representatives and senators at their places dutifully applauding the president after each statement. Although it was exciting to see the president, the Washington Zoo and the Smithsonian Museum provided him with much more enjoyment.

They settled in on the train for their return to Wilmington.

"Jake, what did you think of the president? Wasn't he just great?"

"Well Father, he seemed mighty fine and he certainly had a nice voice, but I tell you, seeing all of those animals at the zoo, now that was great. And the exhibits at the Smithsonian, well, I want to come back soon and look at lots of those things again!"

This trip seemed to begin a closer relationship between father and son. Jake loved his father, but Caleb's job kept him very busy. When Jake was very young he could remember Caleb taking him down in front of the newspaper office on Front Street whenever there was a boxing match. That was before radios were available and fans had to follow the action by waiting for updates from the paper. After each round a press release was posted outside the building detailing the events of the fight. There were editorial guesses as to which fighter prevailed, and further guesses as to how the rounds would total for each fighter. In the event of a knockout, the release was short, but if the fight ended in a total round victory, or a draw, there were many opinions on the matter, resulting in comments and criticism during the weeks to follow. Caleb was excited about this, but Jake took it in stride, just listening to what his father thought. One day after the trip to Washington Caleb made an unexpected announcement to Jake.

"Jake, I think you're old enough and dependable enough for me to introduce you to the wonderful sport of bird hunting."

"Really? Oh Father, that really would be terrific! When can we go? Do you have a gun I can use? I'm right good with my BB gun and I can usually hit the cans I've put on a log when I'm out practicing in the woods." The idea of hunting was so exciting to Jake he could hardly stop for breath.

"Well now don't get too excited. The season doesn't open for a while but when it does we'll take a crack at it," Caleb chuckled.

The dove season opened first but the "bird" season didn't open until November.

In September, as they were enjoying the swing on the front

porch, Jake asked his father, "Since I've heard that the dove season has opened, are we going on a dove shoot? They're birds."

"Well yes Jake, doves certainly are birds, but on a dove shoot you mostly just sit in a field and shoot the dove when and if they fly over. Now 'bird hunting,' that's quite different. I like it because you walk a lot and the season doesn't open until the end of November, so it's cooler. But mainly it's a real joy just watching the dogs work, seeing them take a staunch point when they find a covey of quail. Then you move in to flush up the birds. You can shoot them on the rise . . . oh it's a great thrill."

One crisp, cold Saturday morning after Thanksgiving Caleb and Jake, after checking the guns and dressing warmly, went on the long-awaited quail hunt.

As they walked along in an area where Caleb had permission to hunt he proceeded to give his son some pointers.

"Now son, let me tell you something you need to know about bird hunting. Always be sure you hunt only with people who have been hunting with their fathers. I guess that might sound sort of silly, but I know that once a man has hunted with his father he has been trained right.

"And another thing. I prefer hunting with only one other person. It's safer that way; you have only one person to keep up with and that's important. Guns can be dangerous, but if you take certain precautions they are just fine."

When the dogs went on point Jake did exactly as his father had told him. With a single-barrel shotgun he was able to down his first bird and he was ecstatic. Just watching his son's enjoyment gave Caleb a great deal of pleasure and put a big smile on his face.

In the spring Caleb took Jake fishing with some of his friends and the boy found fishing a great sport—almost as good as hunting. On his initial trip he caught a couple of blues and a puppy drum and he happily brought them home for Carrie to cook for dinner. These outings really enhanced Jake's desire to spend a lot of his time outdoors. He could hardly wait until he owned a shotgun, and fishing rod and reel . . . he just knew he would some day.

As the years passed life went on in the area and at the small school. In December of 1933, to Caleb and Degar's delight, prohibition was abolished and they were now able to obtain a cold beer in many places. A whisky store opened in the middle of town where you could get a bottle for a reasonable price. A statue of a famous Confederate cabinet member was located in the middle of the street with a finger conveniently pointing toward the store.

In the spring of 1927 Lindbergh had flown the Atlantic. Later the tragic story of his son's kidnapping in 1932 had filled many Americans with agitation, grief, and fear. In 1929 the stock market had collapsed, leaving many people who had bet on its continued rise near poverty, causing distress and many suicides across the nation. Banks failed, including the one that held Caleb's funds, but he had been a lucky one, withdrawing his funds before the failure. Franklin Roosevelt was sworn in as president in 1933, and promised to eliminate fear and bring prosperity.

In the early thirties, a small radio station had been started, which gave access to nightly news reports from Lowell Thomas. For the benefit of male listeners the exciting Joe Louis and Jack Sharky fights and other boxing matches were broadcast, being described from ringside blow by blow. The radio provided humor with *Amos 'n' Andy* at evening time, and on Sunday nights there would be Jack Benny with his rather unique brand of comedy. There were other programs enjoyed by adults and young people alike such as the *Lone Ranger*, and *Little Orphan Annie*. The soap operas provided respite for many hard-working, tired housewives. Each week after his inauguration the president would have a fireside chat, hoping to encourage the nation about the economy, saying that things were looking up and would soon get better, and the only thing to fear was "fear itself."

Degar was promoted to assistant foreman, with some increase in pay, but he was still quite unhappy about the disparity between his state and that of the employees in the five-story headquarters building. On one occasion he had worked on the president's car, which was filled with opulent furniture and fixtures, and he had wondered why some people had so much when he struggled to keep and maintain his five-room house and take care of Tess and Ginny.

Tess' life was somewhat better with Degar's raise, but he still had those bad days, and what he didn't take out on the poor dog and Ginny he took out on Tess with abuse and charges of misbe-havior—all of which were untrue and undeserved. She, in order to withstand her situation, began to look elsewhere for the love and devotion she did not receive at home. Jake was at times the object of this interest, although from afar, as was the case in many adolescent affairs.

Caleb's clients had increased very little, and although the Joneses survived, the burden of maintaining 2 Central Boulevard was great. The man who stoked the coal furnace was laid off and this chore became Jake's, as well as the job of shaking down the ashes and cleaning out the grates.

Through those years Jake and Tess had become good friends, walking home from school together and occasionally attending the same school functions. Tess had a few friends, but her best friend was Evelyn Smith who lived close to the Loghins. Jake had three buddies, Ave, Les, and Jack; through the years there were many times when the four boys roamed the woods together and explored as far as the lake to the east and the river to the west. They found out that the snakes and alligators were not as bad as people thought, but they were still cautious. The relationship between the boys and girls at school was rather distant, as it is wont to be at that age because of the difference in their sexes and in their emotional desires. Of course, as they approached the teenage years and entered the maelstrom of adolescence, they more frequently noticed one another. Tess had grown taller, her freckles had become less noticeable, but she still had that vivid red hair. Jake had not grown so much and still had a boyish look that could be a substitute for handsomeness. Both groups began to discuss the new feelings they were experiencing and there was much wonder among them.

They had all been exposed to many books; they were able to endure the teaching, which, under modern standards, was probably inadequate. Two additional rooms and an auditorium had been added to the small, four-room schoolhouse. Because of the additional space their stay at Sunset was extended through the seventh grade. Jake grew to be quite strong, though not very tall, and he was more than able to hold his own in schoolyard fracases. When a group of toughs from the area north of school raided them one day, Jake's friend, Joe Wolf, rescued him from complete defeat by forcibly pulling the large assailant off of Jake and throwing him down—with a warning to not ever come back.

All this time the lure of the lake to the east and the river to the west became more attractive both to the boys and the girls. Many times in their wanderings in the woods or on the riverbank the two groups would have minor confrontations in passing, but the interest and attraction began to grow as nature progressed.

One dark, cold night in 1934 two roundhouse flagmen were directing a locomotive to the proper bay by the use of lanterns. The switch on the track was correctly set and closed. The engine, however, changed directions to another bay. One flagman was on that track and he frantically waved his lantern to warn the engineer. As he tried to get out of the way he tripped and fell. Degar witnessed the oncoming tragedy from the next bay and cried out a warning; the engineer braked but it was too late, the flagman was cut in two by the errant train.

The deceased's family employed Caleb Jones to bring a suit against the railroad to recover compensation, and Degar had been called as a witness. Although he knew compensation was deserved, he was very hesitant in his testimony on the witness stand. This was no doubt caused by his interview with the head of the Legal department, who, soliciting information from him, let it be known very clearly that his attitude and testimony on the witness stand would reflect on his loyalty to the railroad, and on his job.

The jury consisted of good citizens of the town, but most had some connection with the railroad and they ruled in its favor; Caleb lost the case. Degar feared that there would be steps taken against him for testifying, but his fears were unfounded. The head of the Legal department, Bill David, and the trial lawyer handling the litigation were invited to the office of the president for a congratulatory drink after the victory—an honor seldom bestowed. In the elated conversations following, Degar was mentioned as the witness who had probably saved the day. No doubt his testimony had probably influenced the decision to give him a raise.

On the other hand, upon his loss, Caleb's name was once again entered upon the blacklist of lawyers. The railroad tried to make sure no business was ever directed his way. Many lawyers in Wilmington at the time who had sued the railroad suffered a similar penalty.

Chapter Six

Jake had always wanted to build a boat so that he could use it in the lake or on the river. In the late spring he enlisted the help of two of his buddies, Les and Ave, for this project. They started building a small boat in Jake's back yard, behind an overgrown hedge, using yellow pine and nails salvaged from building sites nearby. It was almost ten feet long with two seats and a leeboard of about two feet. They nailed it together in a very square and straightforward manner without benefit of naval architecture. After it was finished, they caulked it by heating old tar and pouring it in the cracks between the boards. All this was done in utmost secrecy, to avoid parental interference and a possible admonition with respect to the "dangers of ships at sea."

Some discussion of this secret venture took place at school, and Tess and her friends, Mary and Evelyn, got wind of it, along with news of its completion and its planned launch in Brown's Lake. The Joneses maid, Carrie, was also aware of it, having witnessed a lot of comings and goings out the back door and behind the hedge. Jake had sworn her to secrecy and was confident that she would hold true.

The boys found some very dark green paint in Ave's garage that would blend with the water grasses in the lake. When they finished painting the boat they dragged it across the road and through the woods to the water. Their friend Jack had joined them that day because it took four people to haul the heavy vessel. Also, Jack owned a paddle, which would surely come in handy. He had found the paddle down by the river where it had washed up after a storm. It was one of his most prized possessions but he happily donated it to become part of the venture.

The boat's christening, without benefit of champagne, was early in the spring, a month before school was out. Tess and Evelyn hid nearby as the boys carried it across the highway to the launching site. With a bottle of grape juice (which they enjoyed first and then filled with water) they christened it *The Rumor* since they knew that others at school were wondering what they were up to.

The launching was muddy and uneventful except for the leaks that appeared in the bottom. This problem was easily alleviated by another application of tar at the site. After making the boat "sea-worthy" the two bravest—Jake and Les—waded out and climbed aboard. With the benefit of Jack's paddle they navigated to the middle of the lake without mishap. Then Jack and Ave swam out to board the punt and at first it seemed to be sufficiently built to hold all four of them. But as the boys climbed in water splashed over the gunwales. All the bailing that followed didn't prevent the would-be sailors from receiving a thorough drenching. *The Rumor* didn't sink, but the boys were soaked. After paddling back and pulling it out of the water they left the punt hidden in the lake grass, planning to combine their boating with a swim when they returned the next day. Tess and Evelyn happened to be walking on the road when the boys returned from the launching, but they ignored them.

"Must not be a very good boat. Did you see how wet they were? It must have sunk," Evelyn said after the boys passed by.

"Well I don't know," replied Tess, "maybe it just wasn't big enough for four guys to be in it at the same time. Besides, we saw where they hid it so if it did sink they were still able to get it to shore."

"Tess, I don't think we should tell anyone about the boat, but let's keep a watchful eye out for what's going on. I'd love to go out on the lake someday. If they take us out we'll promise not to tell anybody where they're hiding it."

It wasn't long before the girls noticed that some of the boys would head into the woods towards the lake every afternoon. They felt that the time was getting ripe for them to see what was going on. One day Evelyn, Mary, and Tess followed the boys into the woods, making sure to stay at a good distance behind them. They walked until they found the path that led to the punt's hiding place. Tess giggled as the other girls tried to keep her quiet. Gradually they crept closer until they could see—to their surprise—the boys skinny-dipping.

"Oh my goodness, they don't have a swimsuit on!" Tess said, but she was too embarrassed to look very closely. Evelyn and Mary were entranced by the sleek, young bodies. Shortly the girls spied the boys' clothes in a pile near where the boat had been launched.

"Let's hide their clothes!" Evelyn said.

"Maybe," replied Mary, "we should hide all of them except one pair of BVDs. That way at least one of them could return partly clothed. We don't want to get them in too much trouble."

Tess started to relax and joined in on the prank. "See that tree over there? Let's toss it high up there. We want them to be able to find it." Before they threw the underwear in the tree the girls waved it in the direction of the boat. They gathered up the clothes and slowly left the scene, knowing that the boys would be unlikely to follow.

The boys heard the commotion, and when they saw the waving BVDs, the panic that ensued almost upended the boat. Swimming, wading, and pulling, they finally managed to bring the boat back to shore. It was Ave's underwear that hung from the tree, but he lived much farther from the lake than Jake.

"Well Jake, since you live the closest guess you'll have to see if you can find our clothes. Ave's underwear can cover you up more than any of us."

"I'll go. If I can't find your clothes I'll bring some of mine; they might not fit but at least you can get home!"

He was a sight to see as he climbed to reach Ave's briefs and then get them on his wet body. He crept along the sandy path— dodging the prickly pears and sandspurs—and when he reached the road he saw the girls running from his yard. He dashed across the road, over the retaining wall, and into the back door.

"Lord, chile! What has you been up to?" chided Carrie. "What'chu got on? Now you boys ain't been skinny-dippin, haz you? I was wondering why somebody had dumped a bunch of clothes on the side porch. I heard Wiggles barking like crazy but I didn't see who it was."

There was no answer from Jake who hastily went to the porch, put on his pants and shirt and shoes, and with an armful of garments headed back into the woods to his grateful friends.

"I can't believe what those girls did. We'll have to get back at them in the worst sort of way," said Jack. Many things were said about the girls, none very complimentary.

The next day at school Tess and Mary, with mischievous gleams in their eyes, quickly slid into their seats. Strangely, their seats seemed sticky. Tess refused to let herself look behind at Jake, which was just as well, because he had his head down and was feigning deep interest in the book on his desk.

When Tess and Mary tried to get up for recess they found that their dresses were stuck to their seats by black caulking tar.

"Mary, Tess, do you have a problem?" asked Miss Bradley, whom you might say was promoted along with the students, for she still taught their class.

"Not really, I guess we must have backed up to something sticky and got it on our dresses," said Mary. Although they made no complaints then, they placed the episode in the back of their minds for future reference.

The boys continued to use and enjoy the boat throughout the summer, but by the time school started the elements had destroyed the vessel. It soon became a happy memory.

Chapter Seven

The class picnic was held at the end of the school year and was particularly important to the members of the seventh grade since they would be leaving for high school the next fall. There was no eighth grade at their school since the Depression had reduced the tax base to the point where it was too costly. Many of the more prosperous parents in town sent their children to preparatory schools to avoid this hiatus in education, but such was not the case for Jake, Tess, and their friends. They were destined to attend the large county high school in town. The end-of-school picnic that year was to be a celebration of their accomplishments thus far.

This year it was to be held at The Cliffs, a high bluff overlooking the river about a mile south of where Central Boulevard reached the riverbank. It was a lovely place about fifty feet high with a sand bank and a beach running down to the tide line. The river at that time was very wide and full from the spring rains; the water had a muddy cast from the red-clay spring runoff of the Piedmont area in the western part of the state.

Tess' food was minuscule, consisting of Vienna sausages and

bread, whereas Carrie had furnished Jake with hot dogs, mustard, pickles, and rolls.

"Dis is too much for jist you. Now you be sure to share some of it with your friends who may not have as much," admonished Carrie that morning before he left.

The crowd walked happily along the river's edge to a spot that was high up and surrounded by pine trees and oaks just starting to show their spring change. They arrived at about four in the afternoon. Soon they settled down with—as usual—the group of girls chatting far apart from the boys.

"Hey everybody, this is a perfect place to have a game of King on the Mountain," said Les. "Let's select sides and have a game."

As they were choosing sides, Jake, Les, and Ave made sure that they were not on the same team as Tess and Evelyn. The boys feared that the tar incident from earlier in the year might come back to haunt them and that they would find themselves at the bottom of the cliff or in the river.

The first engagement ended in a draw. Jake's team then proceeded to the bottom, huddled, and with youthful vigor struggled to the top and began to dislodge those who were defending the summit.

In the tumble that followed many bodies were thrown together, and Jake found that he was tumbling with Tess in his arms. She held on tightly, and the two young buds blooming on her chest, pressing against Jake's chest, were not an unpleasant feeling; in fact, the sensation was pleasing to him, and his potential manhood stirred. He quickly disengaged himself from her embrace and ran to the top of the hill to proclaim victory. Tess breathlessly struggled back up the incline only to find that her team had been defeated and that the remnants of it were still below, without strength to make another assault. She did not understand the feeling of happiness she had had while in Jake's arms.

"Don't cha' think it's time for us to gather up some sticks and broken branches and start a fire? It's getting chilly! Besides, lots of us have hot dogs and we need to roast them!" Les shouted from the bottom of the hill.

They all fanned out and found enough wood to have a good, warming fire as darkness descended. They gathered close around and shared memories of their years in the small school at Sunset Park.

Miss Bradley received praise from all of her students. From the first grade on she had provided guidance for their class. Mrs. Cling, whose brass school bell had been replaced with timed electric bells, was also a topic of discussion. The girls gave Miss Bradley some perfume, and the boys presented Mrs. Cling with a solid brass bell engraved with the word "THANKS" to remind her of her early days at the school.

The evening was nigh, and the fire had burned down to hot embers. The boys cut green sticks for the hot dog roasting. Jake offered the others, including Tess, a stick, a dog, and a bun. When Tess took his offering it made him feel better about throwing her off the cliff.

"Tess," he said as he gave her the hot dog, "I hope you aren't mad because I threw you off the hill. I hope I didn't hurt you." As he was saying this to Tess all he could think about was that pleasant feeling he'd had when they tumbled down the hill.

"Oh, I'm just fine. You didn't hurt me at all."

Later, while sitting on the beach by the fire and singing, they noticed a tugboat slowly pulling a derelict vessel about one hundred feet long up the river.

"Look," said Tess, "they're shoving that old boat towards land." And sure enough it grounded itself slightly north of Central Boulevard. Evidently it was to be abandoned, because the tug picked up speed and disappeared into the darkness that had settled over the river.

"Golly," said Ave, "wonder where that old boat has been? Have you ever wondered what foreign lands the boats on the river might have come from and what the people are like in those places?"

"Well, I wonder about the sailors and who they are and why they like to leave home for a life on the sea. I'm not sure I'd like to be a sailor," responded Jack.

"I wouldn't mind sailing on a ship," said Jake, "but I'm not sure I want to go to those foreign countries. They speak other languages. Now how can you talk to someone who doesn't speak English?"

"I don't know," replied Tess, "it's still fun to dream about them and to think that some day you might travel there. Besides, in a couple of years we'll be taking French or Spanish at high school. Maybe then we could understand them."

Jake turned to Ave and Les. "This summer we'll certainly have to explore this new addition to our shoreline. I don't think *The Rumor* will last very long, so maybe we can fix this old hulk up to enjoy."

Stars were starting to twinkle as a sliver of moon appeared in the sky.

"It's getting to be time to go boys and girls!" Miss Bradley called out. Everyone began to pack up their belongings and the leftover food (of which there was very little) and the picnic ended. Most of the students were rather emotional when expressing their good-byes to Mrs. Cling, and particularly to Miss Bradley.

When Tess returned home it was way after dark. It was nearly nine o'clock and Degar was furious.

"Where have you been and who gave you permission to stay out so late?" he demanded.

"It was the school picnic and you said I could go."

"I didn't know it was to be a night-time picnic. How come you stayed so long? I told you I don't like your associating with some of those kids, they might put ideas in your head. There you were out with them so late. I bet you were just hanging around and associating with some of those bad kids that go to that school."

"But Papa, I'd say that all those people are nice and some of them are especially nice to me. They're my friends."

Whatever Tess said seemed to increase his angry mood and he struck her and sent her to bed with the admonition that she could go on no more school activities without his permission. She knew in her heart that such permission would rarely be given, if at all.

When Jake arrived home he went into the living room to tell his parents good night. "Jake, how was the picnic?" his mother asked.

"Gee Mother, it was just great. We played some games and Jack brought his guitar and we sang—and of course we ate a lot. We watched a tug beach an old boat on the riverbank. It was exciting. I want to go see it tomorrow."

With that he kissed his parents good night and went to his

room. In his lingering thoughts before he drifted off to sleep it puzzled him that it had been so nice with Tess in his arms, and he wondered about the impulse that he felt to kiss her. He had kissed a girl once at a Halloween party when playing Spin the Bottle but he didn't see much to it. She apparently didn't either; when he was bobbing for apples she had dunked his head into the big water tub. He had told his mother that the boat was the exciting moment, but he had to admit that this perplexing Tess problem was even more exciting.

The next morning was the first day of summer vacation and Jake was up early. After breakfast he bounded down the steps to the back yard and checked out all of the things he had stored in the shed behind the house. He suddenly thought of the vessel that had been abandoned on the riverbank. He phoned Ave.

"Hey Ave, how about us going down to look at that old boat the tug left by the river last night? Why don't you come on over and we'll walk to the river and take a look?" Ave came over on his bike and towed Jake, who was on a pair of skates, down to the river. They found the old wooden boat. It was about 120 feet long and beached at a canted angle just below the high tide line. It had formerly been some kind of riverboat, with a small, dilapidated smokestack, a deck cabin, and a roofless pilothouse. The boards on the sides were bent and cracked, and it had long ago lost its seaworthiness. After some difficulty they clambered aboard the slanted deck and made their way into the pilothouse. They found it bare of any equipment except for the remains of the binnacle stand and the broken wooden wheel with spokes missing. They pretended to take control, with Ave as captain and Jake as his first mate. They explored the remainder of the ship, finding old cabins and an engine room devoid of any machinery except the propeller shaft. The name of the boat, *Henry,* was almost obliterated, and the word "Boston" could barely be made out beneath. They left after an hour or so of exploration, vowing to get their buddies together for an imaginary cruise as soon as possible.

As the summer went on the boys decided it might be wise to make some effort to get their group more connected with the girls they had known in school. With that in mind Jake suggested to Evelyn that they all explore the derelict vessel on the beach and she agreed to contact the girls.

On the appointed day they all met at Jake's and walked down to the river. The girls had not seen the abandoned boat in the daylight, and were amazed at its size and the fact that it had been left there. With the help of some ropes Ave had brought along, the six of them scaled the low side and climbed aboard. Ave was elected captain, and Jake was to be the first mate; the others were seamen. With this order of merit they started on their imaginary cruise. They turned the ship to the south and cruised down the river toward the ocean, where in fair and stormy weather they found many distant ports of call. After enduring the dangers of the sea they returned to the reality of being stranded ashore.

The friendly relationships became secure, and Evelyn sort of ended up with Ave, Tess with Jake, and Mary with Les, although the attraction was rather distant at best. They found a stateroom for the captain, and the mate led the girls on a further exploration of the vessel. When Tess and Jake were alone their eyes met for a brief moment.

"Jake, I gotta thank you for being so kind to me." She put her arms around him and invited him to kiss her, which he did with some feeling of enjoyment. Embarrassed, he drew away and tried to resume his disinterested approach. The playful cruise ended with no damage to any of the relationships that were being fostered. In any event, when he returned home he had some satisfaction in the fact that kissing was not so bad after all.

When Jake, Ave, and the others returned to the boat a week later they were met on board by a three-year-old girl in a ragged, dirty dress who was accompanied by a young woman, evidently her mother.

"What do you young people want? Me and my husband and our little girl, Mary, moved into this boat last week. We're living here 'cause we don't have no other place to live. My Bill, he's out of work, so we ain't got no money for a home."

As Mary clutched her mother's knees the woman continued. "He's in town looking for work. I know he don't want any young'uns hanging around, and we'd appreciate you no longer coming aboard. In fact, I hope you'll leave now 'cause he wouldn't like it if you were here when he returns. He's in town looking for work right now, but he'll be coming soon."

As they jumped off the boat they realized that the joy of the abandoned hulk had ended. Jake was particularly disappointed as he had hoped for another kissing engagement, but such was not to be the case. They left just in time to see Bill returning, looking hard in their direction.

When they were walking back, Jake suggested that they stop by his house at the corner and see if Carrie would fix them something cool to drink. They were sitting on the front porch enjoying their drinks and cookies when Carrie suddenly appeared.

"Lord chillun! Wiggles done chased the chicken that I was 'sposed to cook for supper. It's in the back yard with Wiggles close behind. Wish you boys would hep me ketch it."

They all jumped up and ran around to the back of the house where Wiggles was barking, just about to overtake the poor creature. Jake and the others surrounded the bird and they were able to corner it.

"I'll get him," shouted Ave as he grabbed the poor feathered creature. Even holding the bird close to his chest didn't keep him from receiving several pecks on his hands before delivering it to Carrie.

She thanked them and immediately grabbed it by the neck and spun it around until its head separated from its body. The headless bird flopped and fluttered about in the yard.

"My gosh!" exclaimed Les. "That bird doesn't even know it's dead!!"

When it stopped writhing Carrie picked it up by the legs and let the blood drain out and then tossed it into a kettle of boiling water to loosen the feathers before picking it. Despite this lurid scene the youngsters departed for their homes still feeling a full day of pleasure.

The pleasure was short lived for Tess, for when she reached home, Sis was limping and Degar was in a bad mood. Those wonderful feelings of the day drifted away.

Sometime later Jake saw an article in the local paper that the welfare department had removed a homeless family from the abandoned vessel and had placed the little girl in a foster home. It also stated that the ship would be burned, and when Jake went back to the river's edge there was nothing left but a few blackened ribs and the partially-burned keel.

Chapter Eight

J ake and his friends entered the high school on Market Street with the same anticipation that they had upon entering the first grade. They tried to act as though they'd been there a long time, but their excitement made it very obvious that they were new students. Many of them were in the same homeroom, including Jake and Tess. Miss Montgomery, their teacher, made the usual new-semester welcome with the same time-worn admonitions that they were to behave well, attend all classes, and do their homework. Much to Jake's chagrin his father insisted that he take Latin every year in high school. It turned out to be a subject which was in no way compatible with his learning or speaking abilities, and with which he struggled over those four years.

As they got older, the relationships between the boys and girls grew, as is apt to happen when the hormones of adolescence begin to blossom. The boys increasingly found themselves more attracted to the girls, and at recess, what had formerly been separate groups had become pairs. Jake and Tess followed this natural process and frequently they could be seen sitting at a table in a corner of the cafeteria deep in conversation.

One day Jake started to talk about his summer plans. "You know, I enjoy my summers but I'd like to get a summer job. I'd like to be a lifeguard at the beach. I might be too young now, but maybe when I'm sixteen . . . . I love being outdoors, and what better job could you have to be outside?"

"Jake, that sounds wonderful. I know you'd make a really good lifeguard. I've seen you swim. You're a good swimmer!"

"Knowing how to swim isn't all a lifeguard needs to know, but it's a start. Wouldn't you like to get a summer job too?"

"Oh I would, but I don't know what I could do. There aren't many jobs for girls, Jake."

"Yeah, I know. When I finish high school I plan to go to college and after that, I hope to go to law school and become a lawyer like my father. I want to live in a place where I can enjoy hunting and fishing just like my father."

"I guess you'll be able to go to college. I know I never will."

"Oh come on, Tess, why not?"

"In the first place I don't think Papa would send me. He's still so awful to me. Even if he could afford it I don't think he would."

"Why not? You're the only child he has!"

"Well, he's always talking about not making much money and you know how he wants me to take care of things at home. If I go off to school Ginny will have to do all the work and she really doesn't like to do it. To keep peace with her Papa makes me do most everything! And when I don't do it fast enough, or the way he wants me to, he's mean, he yells at me, and sometimes he even hits me!"

"Oh Tess, I knew things weren't good for you but I didn't

55

know he'd ever hit you. That's terrible! I wish there were some way I could help you. Maybe—"

"No Jake, I wouldn't want you to do anything. You don't know what an awful temper he has. No telling what he would do if he knew I'd told someone about the way he treats me," Tess said.

"Can't Ginny do anything?"

"Well she's scared of him so she's not gonna cross him."

As they parted Jake gave her hand a squeeze. "I still wish I could do something, just something."

Jake went back to class thinking about how Tess' father treated her. It was hard for Jake to understand that a father could be so mean to his daughter. He thought about how lucky he was that he had kind and loving parents. When he needed discipline they didn't hesitate to correct him in some manner, but they were never unfair or mean and had never beaten him.

Now and then Jake and Tess would go to the corner drug store to share a soda whenever Jake could save a quarter. These were the times when their relationship became more endearing. Tess appreciated how nice he was to her, and it made him feel good to see her smile.

Because the school was so small the proms were open to all of the students. The lowerclassmen could attend for a small fee. Jake and Tess had conferred about this, and by saving a little lunch money and Jake being paid for odd jobs around the house, they were able to go to the prom in the spring of 1936. As Jake was too young to drive, Caleb volunteered to take them to and from the gymnasium.

On the big night Caleb drove Jake to Tess' house. She ran out the door.

"Hi Jake, Hello Mr. Jones."

Jake gave her a carnation corsage, which she clipped on her wrist.

"Oh Jake, it's beautiful! And it smells so good. Thank you! No one has ever given me flowers before."

Jake opened the door for her, as his father had told him to do, and the two of them got in and sat on the back seat in silence.

As soon as they got to the gym they were chatting happily. The music was good and a lot of the dancers enjoyed jitterbugging. During the last piece of the evening—Hoagy Carmichael's "Stardust"—Tess teared up as she told Jake that Degar had threatened her again.

"He was so angry when I left. He didn't want me to come to the dance."

"Golly, Tess, I'm so sorry. What did he say?"

"'Tess if you don't stop going 'round with those kids and don't pay more attention to my needs here at home there'll be hell to pay!' I dunno, but sometimes I'm really scared."

"He said that? I wonder what he meant?"

It was evident that the relationship between father and daughter was becoming more and more difficult. It seemed to Jake that Tess feared for her life. As she continued to tell him how stressful her life was, Jake tried to gently dry her tears. "I love you Tess," he said suddenly.

Tess, still somewhat damp faced, lit up. "You're the only one who's told me that in a long, long time." But by the time Caleb picked them up to drive them to Tess' house, the two couldn't stop talking and laughing about their wonderful evening.

In those days the high school was about four miles from Central Boulevard so the students out in Sunset Park were issued tickets to ride the trolley back and forth. There was no turntable at Central Boulevard and Adams Street where the tracks ended. This meant that at the end of the line the conductor had to get out, walk around to the back, and switch the trolley pole to the north end. Re-boarding, he would flip the backs of the seats and move the portable throttle to the new front end of the car to get everything in place for the trip back to the north. The passengers, patiently waiting during this operation, would climb in with the call of "All a-bo-ard!" The devices involved in switching directions provided mischief for some of the boys on the trolley. At times one of them would slip to the back of the car as it was moving, reach through the back window, grab the rope holding the trolley pole, and pull it, which immediately caused the trolley to stop. The conductor would once again disembark, go to the rear, and replace the trolley pole on the wire. While he was busy doing this, other troublemakers might dump the sand box, which was aboard in case of an emergency. The students called the regular conductor "Soda Water." He was good humored and took these shenanigans in stride. But one day a new conductor was aboard, and he reported their mischief to the company, which in turn reported it to the principal of the school, who wrote a letter to all the students' parents. In due time, both Caleb and Degar received these letters. Tess truthfully denied any participation, but Jake had to reluctantly admit involvement. Degar didn't believe Tess and further castigated her for being with "that crowd." Jake lost his allowance for two weeks.

That summer Jake spent most of his time at the beach, but he didn't get the dreamed-for job. The others each went their own way. Occasionally they would see each other in the neighborhood, but they had no regular get-togethers as they had in the past. Tess tried to please Degar with her work around the house, but he increasingly placed more on her—and even seemed to resent her presence.

Chapter Nine

In early May 1936, it was near bedlam in the Freight Traffic department at the railroad. Several boxcars, which had been loaded in town with cotton from the Compress Warehouse, had been sent north on the main line to Richmond and, from there, transferred to the C&O for delivery in Cincinnati. Near the West Virginia border the train had derailed and three cars were stranded off the tracks, one overturned.

The president, Mr. Ellian, had heard about it in a radio report the evening before and had assembled Mr. David of the Legal department, Mr. Cole of Freight Traffic, and Mr. Groover of the Engineering department to discuss the matter and determine what should be done.

"Well gentlemen, let's hear your ideas concerning this most unfortunate event."

"The cotton is due at the mill in two days," said Mr. Cole, "and if we don't deliver by then there will be demurrage and loss of freight revenue. The cotton bales, if they haven't been damaged, could be delivered by other means, but this must be done as soon as possible."

"I think we should send someone to the site to look into the legal aspects of the matter, and—"

Mr. Ellian interrupted. "Mr. David, I don't want to hear any legal jargon at this time. Responsibilities can be sorted out at a later date."

After further discussion it was decided that a delegation from the Freight Traffic department, the Engineering department, and the Maintenance department—together with Mr. Cole— would go to the site as soon as possible. At about noon, Jere Swain and Degar Loghin were notified that they were to accompany Mr. Cole to the site. They prepared to take the train that afternoon in order to reach the wreck the next day. Cole was assigned to a sleeper, but Degar and Jere were assigned to a passenger car, which meant they would have to sit up all night. As they walked to their accommodations the importance of the mission became apparent; they saw that the president's private car was being attached to end of the train. Evidently he felt that his presence in Cincinnati was required.

After a very uncomfortable night in the day-coach the train arrived in Richmond at an early morning hour and the three men were transferred by car to the old C&O station. They noted that Mr. Ellian's private car was switched over so as not to disturb his sleep. They stopped at the station grill for a cup of coffee as they awaited the call for the train to Cincinnati. When they boarded the train they found their seats and immediately went to the diner for a hearty breakfast.

"You know, we need to plan a trip to go floundering this fall," Jere said when they were settled in their day-coach seats.

"I'd love to do that, but I haven't had a Saturday off in a 'coon's

61

age. No way I can go fishing when I have to work six days a week."

"Well maybe someday you'll get a Saturday off. Why don't we go ahead and plan and then when we have the chance we'll be ready?" After discussing the fishing plans the conversation took a turn.

"Jere, I not only have to work my butt off, but things are awful at home. I need some time off sumthin' terrible."

"What's wrong at home? What do you mean?"

"Well, you know, Tess, she seems to be feeling her oats . . . she's hard to manage, sasses me all the time, complains about her chores. I just don't know what to do with her. And then there's Ginny, always with a pitiful face, whining all the time 'cause she wants a baby. I told her when we married there'd be no more children, but she still frets about it almost all the time. And to top it all off they both stay half sick a lot, mostly seem to have bad stomachs."

"If they're sick so much you might want to get some insurance in case one of 'em has a serious illness, maybe needs an operation or something. Those of us that work for the railroad can have medical attention through the Surgeon General, but I think it's awful that there's no outside insurance provided for families."

"Wouldn't that cost a lot of money? The insurance, I mean?"

"May not. I've heard that there's a man in the Freight Traffic department who sells insurance on the side and that you can purchase small amounts for as little as seventy-five cents a week."

"That sounds like a good idea. I'll have to remember that. I think I can afford a small policy; maybe I can get one for them together. After we get back maybe you can find out his name for me."

It was a hot muggy day when the train finally puffed into Cincinnati. After getting off they were told that the crash site was several miles away. They climbed into a car and were transported to the overturned locomotive and many derailed and smashed freight cars. They located the cars loaded with the cotton in about the middle of the train. One of them was damaged beyond repair, but the cotton was salvageable. They arranged for the cotton to be off-loaded and taken by truck to its destination in Cincinnati. Degar and the engineer arranged for the wrecked car to be salvaged, with the railroad receiving credit for any proceeds. The remaining cars were removed by crane to a sidetrack nearby and pulled to the shops of the C&O. Degar and Jere went to the shop so that Degar could attend to any necessary repairs and Jere could arrange salvage for the damaged cotton. It turned out that this couldn't be done quickly; in fact it required spending one, maybe even two nights.

Degar and Jere registered in a small downtown hotel named the York. After taking their suitcases to the room Degar cleaned up and they went out on the town. They checked out every bar and dive they thought the expense account could cover. They finally got hungry and decided to have dinner at the A & B Restaurant not far down the street. Degar was rather taken with their waitress, a small brunette named Eliza Harper. She pushed her affections on him, and she agreed when Degar suggested that they get together later. At closing time Jere went back to the hotel alone and Degar and his new friend went off in another direction.

When Degar returned several hours later with the smell of liquor on his breath and perfume on his clothes, Jere knew he had been up to no good. Degar struggled out of bed the next morning at seven o'clock with a terrible headache.

"All I've got is a small bottle of bicarbonate of soda that I brought up here. I need more than that. I gotta have some aspirin, and a lot of it; this is a humdinger! Guess I'll get dressed and see if I can find a drug store. Hope they'll be open this early."

"I remember seeing one yesterday. It's only a couple of blocks down the street from the hotel."

Jere waited in the lobby for Degar, who finally appeared with a bag in his hand.

"Let's go in and eat. I'm hungry."

"I need to take my bag upstairs."

"Don't you want to take the aspirin with you?"

"Yeah, but I bought more than one tin. I'd like to take it upstairs."

After Degar returned they ate breakfast and headed for the wreck site. Jere arranged for the cotton to be transshipped to a recycle gin nearby. Mr. Cole confirmed the transaction by phone and promised to transfer the necessary funds.

Degar's work was not so simple. The air systems on the cars were disabled from the derailment. Despite his rather unstable condition he was an excellent mechanic and was able to negotiate the necessary repairs. The railroad was able to save the cars and use them again.

After finishing their jobs Degar and Jere faced more uncomfortable travel on the hot day-coach. As they were leaving the station, Jere noticed that Eliza was nearby to tell Degar good-bye. The next day, though tired and worn out from the trip, they arrived back home in time to go to work at their respective positions.

When Degar reached home that evening he was in one of his outrageous moods. He gave Sis a kick on the left leg, went into the house, and then scolded Tess for imagined behavior in his absence; he demanded that Ginny prepare his supper and left for the nearest bar.

Shortly after Degar returned from the trip to Cincinnati, Sis began to show her age. Degar told Tess he had given her worm pills. One day when Tess got home from school Sis was in a state of convulsion and her legs were stiff and extended. Tess tried to get her to drink some water and comfort her, but to no avail.

Early the next morning when she was leaving for school, Tess found Sis lying dead in the yard. Tess covered her with an old burlap bag. Sis had been her friend.

She told Jake about it when she got to school. "Jake, our old hound dog Sis died last night. I want to bury her when I get home this afternoon but I can't do it alone. Do you think you could help me?"

"Gee Tess, I'm so sorry about Sis. Losing your dog is hard. I know it was when Wiggles died. I'll be glad to help. Why don't I come to your house, say, at about 3:30?"

"Thank you. She meant a lot to me, but I know Papa wouldn't bother to bury her. I really appreciate it, Jake."

"Do you know why she died?"

"No. It could have been old age with the way she's been acting lately . . . but she really wasn't that old for a dog. We have a shovel so you don't have to bring one. Guess I'll see you around 3:30?"

"Yeah, I'll be there."

When Jake arrived at Tess' house he was carrying a large box. "I stopped by the store and picked up this box. Thought we might need it to put her in."

"I already have her wrapped up in this old burlap bag. Don't ya think we could take her across the road and bury her in the woods? She liked to run over there and chase rabbits."

"Do you think she ever caught one?"

"Naw, I don't think she did; least ways she never brought one home."

Jake picked up the burlap sack, put Sis in the box, and started across the road.

"When Wiggles got run over I buried him somewhere near here I think. Let's go into the woods now and find a place."

About fifty yards into the woods there was a shaded sandy hill and Tess stopped. "This looks like a good spot here. It should be easy to dig since it's sandy."

"I think we should bury her about three feet deep. That way no foxes or other animals can dig her up," Jake said. With that, he proceeded to dig a hole about two by four feet and at least three feet deep. They took Sis, still wrapped up in the burlap bag, out of the box and put her into the hole. Tess created a little mound and placed pine straw over it and then she marked the spot with a board sort of shaped like a cross. Tess said her last good-bye. "I'll miss you, Sis. You know, my daddy never did like this dog and used to kick her when he got home. But she was a good dog and I'll miss her. Sis was the only one at the house that was always glad to see me when I came home. I guess she loved me. I know I loved her."

With Tess' good-byes over, they started walking back to her house hand in hand.

"Jake, you're my best friend. If I knew how to love you, I would, but I guess we're too young to do that anyway." She took him in her arms and kissed him. "That's my thanks for your help."

They continued their slow walk towards Tess' home enjoying their closeness. When they arrived at the house, Ginny was sitting on the front porch, and Jake could see that she had been crying.

"Guess I better head for home. I'll be seeing you Mrs. Loghin. See you in school, Tess."

Tess sat down by Ginny. "What's the matter Ginny? You look like you've been crying."

"Oh, I have Tess. You see, I'm gonna have a baby and I'm afraid your daddy is going to be really mad. He doesn't want any more children. Now don't you tell anyone 'cause he don't want people knowing his business."

"I won't tell anyone Ginny, I promise."

"Tess, I want you to swear you won't tell."

"I swear."

"You swear what?"

"I swear I won't tell anyone that you're going to have a baby."

"Thanks Tess, that makes me feel better."

Chapter Ten

Another child had been a constant source of contention in the Loghin household. Tess had frequently witnessed Degar's anger at Ginny's desire to have a child. When Ginny's father visited he often expressed his hope that he would be blessed with a grandchild.

"It's none of your Pop's business whether we have a child or not. You tell him to shut his mouth," Degar would shout when his father-in-law was gone.

"But Degar—"

"No buts about it Ginny. No more talking about grand-children!"

One day when Degar got home Ginny went into the kitchen and got him a beer. She also prepared him his favorite dinner: spare ribs, collards, and potatoes.

"Well Ginny, what's this all about . . . serving me a beer and my favorite dinner?"

"Degar," Ginny said smiling, "don't get mad, but we're going to have a baby. I hope by now you'll agree that it's time and that it's all right!"

"Maybe you're right, Ginny, and I guess Tess will be pleased." But inside Degar seethed with rage, envisioning the additional expense and inconvenience.

On the Sunday after Degar's return and the revelation of the baby he suggested a family trip to South Beach, which was about fifteen miles from where they lived. The trip was bumpy in the old car but they arrived safe and sound to join the crowds of vacationers in the resort area. This was a working man's beach, with lots of small concessions and stores providing entertainment and cheap merchandise. Degar went for a swim while Tess and Ginny stayed on the beach absorbing the rays of the summer sun.

"I'm beginning to feel queasy in the morning," said Ginny. "The doctor gave me some pills to help, but they don't seem to do much good. Degar said he would ask the dispensary at the railroad if they have something that could help me."

"Well, I hope the pills will make you feel better. Ginny, look. See the guy waving? That's Les, he's a friend of mine at school. Think I'll go see what he's up to."

Les was glad to see her and they decided to take a swim together and headed for the ocean. Upon entering the breakers Degar confronted them and told Tess to go back and watch over Ginny. Afterwards, Tess and Ginny took a short swim together and had lunch. They ate hot dogs with mustard and onions at a small concession stand that smelled of recent cooking and had a "B" for its sanitation grade. The young man behind the counter looked as though he hadn't bathed in a couple of days and kept looking hungrily at Tess. She returned his look, but shifted her eyes when Degar reprimanded her. The day ended with the slow ride back home at twilight, and the ultimate bed-tossing heat of the summer night.

The next morning Ginny was actively sick at breakfast. Her face was ashen when she returned to the table.

"Ginny, when I get to work I'll check by the dispensary and see if they can give me something to help your morning sickness," Degar told her. He went to Tess' room before he left. "You get up. Ginny is sick. You clean this house good and don't you leave it. Somebody needs to look after Ginny, and that somebody is you!"

Later Jake came by and they sat on the front porch and talked while Ginny suffered inside.

"Papa took us to the beach yesterday. I had a good time, but he was watching me all the time. I saw Les and we were going for a swim, but just as we were going in Papa was coming out and he glared at Les and told me to tend to Ginny. But it was still fun. We had hot dogs before we came home."

"I'm sorry Ginny's sick. Maybe the hot dogs didn't agree with her."

"No. That's not it. She's going to have a baby. Sometimes women are sick in the morning when they're going to have a baby. Oh goodness! I swore to Ginny I wouldn't tell anyone. Jake you won't tell, will you? Jake, please, promise?"

"I promise, Tess. I won't tell. Maybe it will be good to have a baby in the house—maybe it will soften up your father a bit."

"I sure hope so . . . I could use a little good and a little softening in the house."

"Would you like to take a walk down to the river?"

"Oh, I can't do that! Papa told me to stay with Ginny," Tess said, and they parted company.

When Degar returned that evening he placed a small bottle of pills on the kitchen table and told Ginny that if she felt bad she should take one with her meals. She took the first one at supper that night. He was particularly solicitous about her health, and Tess was surprised at the compassion he was showing; it was a far cry from his usual behavior. She hoped that Jake was right and that having a baby in the house might be a good thing. This continued for the next day or two, and Ginny appeared to be suffering less from her condition. Tess noticed that the label on the bottle said it was some kind of bicarbonate of soda and she was glad that it seemed to be helping Ginny.

June passed on into July, and Ginny began to show. She continued to take the pills and they seemed to make her more comfortable. However, one mid-July breakfast, when they were eating their usual grits and sausage, Ginny became violently ill. When they called the doctor he advised them to take her to the hospital. At the hospital she began to have convulsions and they decided to pump out her stomach. After this procedure she got better, and two days later she returned home and resumed her usual life of cooking for Degar and Tess. This continued for about a week, with Degar being more and more solicitous about Ginny's health and the approaching birth.

On a late July morning Ginny's symptoms reappeared and when Degar was notified he immediately brought a doctor to the house to examine her. Degar showed him the bottle of pills and told him that the bicarbonate of soda was all that she had taken that morning. The doctor thought that she might have heart trouble and suggested that they take her to the hospital again. Before they could even call an ambulance she had several more violent seizures. Her hands and feet became rigid and contracted, and she died at about seven o'clock that evening. Degar called the undertaker, who came immediately, and he also noted her rigid condition. She was taken to the mortuary, and following a church service one day later she was buried in the local cemetery.

It seemed to Tess that Degar wasn't too upset over Ginny's death—although he did buy flowers and place them on her grave. He also told Tess that he had ordered a small monument to place on the grave. A few days later he appeared rather happy, and from what Tess had overheard on the telephone, he had collected on a small insurance policy on Ginny's life that had covered the burial expenses.

Afterwards Degar came in late each evening smelling of liquor and demanding that Tess fix his dinner with the meager amount of food he kept in the house. On a Thursday night in August, following the burial, he did not come in for supper and Tess went to bed at about ten o'clock. Sometime in the early morning she suddenly awoke to the smell of alcohol and perfume and was aware of someone in bed with her. A leg was thrown over her leg, a hand started probing between her legs, and an arm was slung heavily over her midriff. She struggled to get away from the grasp, ran to the bathroom, and locked the door. Degar—who was quite intoxicated—beat on the door and begged her to come out, promising to go to bed and not bother her anymore. "Come on out Tess. I promise not to bother you again. Come on out Tess." She refused, and finally she heard him leave and close his bedroom door. She went back to her room thoroughly shaken, and although she tried, she couldn't get back to sleep.

Getting up early, dressing hurriedly, and skipping breakfast, she left the house and headed for town. She didn't know where she was going, but she didn't want to stay at home. When she boarded the streetcar "Soda Water" gave her a smiling welcome. Jake was seated nearby, but she hardly spoke to him and sat across the way. He wondered why she was so aloof and distraught. Tess wondered if she should tell someone about what Degar had done but decided not to—not now anyhow.

Chapter Eleven

Degar's schedule at the railroad finally opened up enough for him and Jere to go fishing. It was an early October morning and the tide was reaching its high at about half past three. It was best to go floundering at high tide when the sandy beach along the shore would be covered with clear fall water and the flounder could be seen from the surface.

Degar left home at about two o'clock in the morning and took the trolley to the beach car stop near Jere's house. He hadn't waited long before he saw Jere carrying a couple of buckets, a Coleman lantern, waders, and two flounder gigs—five-foot staffs headed by three-forked gaffs. The gigs were used to spear the flounder as it lay in the shallows of the sound near the beach.

"Morning, Degar. Guess the beach car will be along soon. I've already reserved a small boat at the dock. Once we get to the dock, we'll pole the boat along the edge of the marsh to the channel next to the beach. At high tide the flounder lie in wait for the bait fish," Jere said.

"Great! I can hardly wait. Here, let me help you with all that fishing gear. Looks like you've thought of everything that we could possibly need."

As Degar helped Jere the beach car appeared around the bend and they boarded with all their gear in tow. The tracks for the ride to the beach ran through a rather affluent part of town. The owner of the car line had acquired the property on each side of the track, which meant that in time he would profit from the development of those areas—in fact he was doing so rather handily already. The line had been part of the Insull Dynasty, which had been broken up a few years earlier and resulted in a local monopoly of the transportation, gas, and electric business in the area. About ten miles down the tracks they reached the trolley station along the shore of the sound. It was located just before the tracks entered the trestle over the wide marshland between the mainland and the island known as North Beach.

They alighted in darkness and walked a short way along a small channel to the pier where the "a-dollar-a-day" boats were available. They paid for the boat and picked up a couple of poles about six feet long for pushing it along. They traveled slowly down a narrow channel towards the beach and came to a place where it widened and became sandy at the bottom. After some pumping and swearing they lit the Coleman lantern and suspended it from a small boom on the bow of the boat. It was about half a mile from the landing to North Beach and they proceeded slowly. When they arrived at the beach Jere eased into the water and walked along the right side of the boat carrying one of the gigs. Degar stayed in the boat and poled the boat beside him. The cool October morning made the work easy. Suddenly Jere stopped.

"Look Degar, see that faint, sorta dark image embedded in the sand?"

"Where? Where? All I see is a shadow."

Before Degar could get his words out Jere had plunged his gig into the shadow. When he pulled it up there was a small flounder of three or four pounds struggling on the end of the gig. Jere flipped the fish into a bucket and took a stringer from his pocket. With impressive speed he slipped the stringer through the fish's gill and out of its mouth, looping it and suspending the flounder from the rear of the boat.

"If we put the fish in the water they'll keep better and be fresher when we get them home."

"That sure makes sense. But I never would have thought that that shadow was a fish. I must say, it surely was shaped like a flounder but I didn't think about that. I can't wait to try my hand at gigging me one."

"First let me show you a time or two how to use the gig, you know, so you'll really see how to do it."

After several spearings by Jere it was Degar's turn with a gig. He made a few futile attempts, then finally speared a five or six pounder.

"Hey, this ain't bad. I never really knew why flounder at the fish market always seem to have holes in 'em. Now I know. I sure hope we can get some more."

They continued to pole and gig along the channel bank. As they were nearing the southern inlet they both noticed that daylight was rapidly approaching.

From time to time, in addition to the flounder, they had seen bait fish of all sorts darting in the water, fleeing from the disturbance of the boat. Occasionally the smooth surface of the water would be broken by silver splashes, as a predator attacked a school of fall mullet.

"Degar, we have a cast net in the boat. If we throw it out we could probably get a lot of bait fish and we could sell 'em and make enough to pay for our morning of fishing."

At that suggestion Degar tossed the cast net and they pulled in half a bucketful, which pleased them both.

With the sun well above the horizon they headed back north, and as they poled along, they looked across the way and saw a boathouse where a man with a chauffeur's cap was lowering a sleek mahogany Chris Craft into the water. Shortly a man appeared from a house nearby and seated himself in the boat's stern. The chauffeur headed the boat toward the mainland. They passed the two fishermen at a high rate of speed, nearly swamping the smaller boat as it was being poled along. Both Degar and Jere immediately recognized the man as Mr. Ellian, the president of the Atlantic Coast Line. His personal steward was acting as captain and wore the chauffeur's cap, and they headed for the railroad boat landing where the president's automobile was parked and waiting.

Degar cursed the two of them. "That boat must have cost that S.O.B. a fortune, and imagine, he just sits back and lets someone run it for him. I don't understand why those who haz seem to git more." With that their delightful morning of fishing soured somewhat. A smoldering resentment had been growing in both of them because of their different financial circumstances. No doubt it would continue to grow.

When they arrived at the landing the other fishermen admired the catch they carried in their bucket. They received about a dollar for the fish bait and that meant their morning trip was doubly pleasing. These two events lifted their low moods, and in celebration Degar broke out a small bottle of "white lightening".

They began to drink at the dock and continued after they boarded the beach car for the return trip to town. Jere got off near his home, but Degar stayed on until the car reached Main Street where he received a transfer slip for the car going toward his home. Since it was early in the afternoon he went to the nearest bar at the Orton Hotel, where he knew there was a pretty girl to flirt with and a supply of the latest moonshine.

There he met Eliza Harper who had recently arrived from Ohio and had a job in the restaurant. They sat at the bar a while and after whispered conversation went to a room in the hotel where the tired, recently-widowed fisherman enjoyed her company and affections throughout the early afternoon.

That same morning Jake had called Tess. "There's an old Tom Mix show on at the Bijou. Would you like to see it?"

"It must be an old film, but I think it would be fun to see a cowboy movie again. Papa's not here to stop me, so I'd love to go."

They took the streetcar in time for the one o'clock show. It was a typical Wild West tale with Tom Mix holding forth as the hero and lover combined. It was nice sitting close to Tess in the darkness, and the warmth of her body next to him permeated Jake with feelings that he enjoyed and found hard to describe. He held her hand, and she cuddled up to him in response to an exciting scene. Afterwards they enjoyed a coke at the soda shop and then boarded the streetcar for the trip back home.

When the car had gone about two blocks Tess suddenly

jumped up and, without a word, left Jake and took a seat on the other side of the car. Jake soon realized why she left so abruptly. As they pulled up to the next stop he saw Degar carrying a package wrapped in newspaper and talking to a brightly-dressed woman. He'd obviously been drinking, and he stumbled into the car and sat down. He didn't see Tess right away, but when he spotted her he immediately went over and sat down next to her.

"What ya doin' here?" he slurred.

"I came into town to look around since there was no one at the house."

"Well I see that boy from the big house on Central Boulevard on the trolley, and I bet you two have been messing 'round."

"We only went to a movie and had a soda."

"I've told you not to mess around with these boys in the neighborhood. When you git home you'll clean these fish and git the house straightened out, or you'll wish you were dead." He turned to Jake. "You keep away from my daughter. She has enough to do taking care of me without associating with the likes of you," he said with a sneer.

This scene ruined the day for Tess and Jake, and at the end of the line Tess quickly descended from the car and ran toward home. Jake tried to speak to her, but she was too far down the street for conversation, and he avoided any confrontation with Degar.

When Tess reached the house, she threw the paper-wrapped fish into the kitchen sink, went to her room, and locked the door. When Degar came in he knocked on her door. When she refused to let him in he took off his belt, broke down the door, and flailed her with his belt. She ran as quickly as possible from the house and went to Evelyn's house about a block away. Evelyn's mother, Mrs. Smith, met her at the door.

"Oh Tess, what's happened? What's the matter?" When she saw the red marks on Tess' arms and legs she tried to comfort her. Tess tearfully related the story of Degar's abuse and threats. Mrs. Smith called Degar and told him that Tess was going to spend the night.

The next morning she tried to talk to Tess. "Tess, I think you should talk to someone at the city welfare department. I'm calling to see—"

"Oh please, Mrs. Smith! Don't do that. Papa will be furious. I don't know what he would do!"

"Now, now Tess, you shouldn't have to put up with this, even if he is your father. I'm sure they can help him mend his ways."

After much persuasion Tess finally agreed to see someone at the welfare department. The appointment was set up for the following Monday, but in the meantime Tess returned home. Degar was remorseful, really quite respectful and solicitous, even taking her to the cafeteria for Sunday dinner after they attended a church service together.

After school on Monday Mrs. Smith picked up Tess and took her to the county courthouse. She was introduced to Miss Jane Acres, a middle-aged matronly woman with a kind smile who told Tess that she would listen to her story and try to help her. Tess related everything with respect to her treatment, Ginny's painful death, Degar's alcoholism, his beatings. She very reluctantly told Miss Acre about the beating that had convinced her to run away.

Jane Acre started on a long monologue, beginning with the admonition that all children should respect and love their parents. "You know Tess, I guess your daddy is missing Ginny. Maybe he was just trying to comfort and console you; in his way he was trying to let you know he loved you. I'm sure he knows what's best for you since he's raised you, and I'm sure he has loved you all your life. Little differences occur in most families but that doesn't indicate a lack of love. Things like this usually result in a continuing and lasting love. Now, I want you to go home and tell your daddy that you love him. Try to take the place of Ginny by fixing him meals when he's home. Just try to be a good daughter."

"But Miz Acres, he's so mean to me."

"Is he mean to you all the time?"

"Well . . . no."

"I thought so. Now Tess, life can be hard. Remember he's taken care of you your whole life. Money has been tight and that fact alone can make the breadwinner very cross. I'm sure he's worried about how to take care of his responsibilities. Just remember he's your father and treat him like you'd like to be treated, that's a good rule to live by. I wish you well, Tess. I'll drop by tomorrow and I want you to call me in a month or so."

Mrs. Smith and Evelyn were disappointed in the outcome of the visit. As they left Mrs. Smith gave Tess a hug. "Well honey, I guess she knows best since she helps families, but I wish something could be done. You just come on home with us now and we'll have a real nice dinner before you go home."

"Oh thank you, Miz Smith. All I really want to do is to travel to my grandmother's house in South Carolina. I never want to live with Papa again!"

After supper Mrs. Smith took Tess home and confronted Degar about his abuse.

The next day Jane Acre went by the house to see Tess and insisted that Degar tell his daughter that he loved her, which he did in a repentant sort of way. For a while things were better after that, and Degar became very solicitous of her needs. Once again Degar hid the seething rage he felt inside.

About a week later Tess arrived home and found Degar sitting in the living room with the brightly-dressed woman she had seen with him the week before at the trolley stop.

"Tess, this is Miz Harper. She's been living downtown. She has agreed to come to our house and help with the housekeeping, which will take some of the duties off of you. I hope it will make your life better."

Tess managed a polite reply and retired to her room, wondering what in the world was going on. She was enlightened shortly thereafter when Ms. Harper arrived at the house with a suitcase and moved herself and her belongings into Degar's room. At first she helped some with the daily routine, including the preparation of the evening meal. Soon however, Eliza became lackadaisical, staying in the house all day listening to soap operas on the radio and poring over the contents of the latest movie magazines. Eliza and Tess' relationship was strained at best, but Degar enjoyed Eliza's presence. Judging from the sounds emanating from the bedroom at night their relationship was more than friendly.

On one occasion Eliza confronted Tess about going to the county offices to complain about her father. Eliza claimed it had upset Degar horribly. Tess realized then that although he had been more civil to her, Degar resented her being around. She was always fearful in his presence, and said as much to Jake.

Chapter Twelve

Eliza Harper had come to town shortly after Degar's trip to Ohio. She got a job at the Orton Hotel, and since they provided rooms for their employees, she moved in with two other restaurant workers. Degar had clandestine meetings with her frequently after she arrived in Wilmington. Eliza was a widow and Degar had suggested that she come and keep house for him, hinting that he would like to marry her. After Tess filed her complaint against him, he propositioned Eliza again and she agreed; Degar hoped that she would help him with his relation-ship with Tess. Eliza moved into his house and they lived as man and wife. This brought some tranquility to the household, as Eliza acted as a buffer between Degar and Tess.

Fall arrived and Jake and Tess began their junior year at school. As Thanksgiving approached, Tess looked forward to the short holiday. Jake had invited her to do a little jukebox dancing on Friday. She acquired a new dress with Eliza's help, and although Degar objected, she was still planning to go.

On Thanksgiving Day Tess and Eliza prepared a turkey dinner with all the trimmings, including sweet potato pie. Degar was drinking, but he hung around the kitchen, and when the cooking was finished they all sat down to dinner together. Tess noticed that Degar had the bottle of pills that had been around before Ginny's death.

"Tess, since you've finished dinner you should take one of these pills. I got 'em from the doc at the railroad. He said they aid in digestion. Good digestion is necessary for good health, you know. Why don't ya take one or two now? How about you Eliza? You could take a couple as well."

"Papa, I don't think I need 'em."

"That's being dumb. If they help, you should take 'em!"

"But I'm fine Papa, I don't need—"

"*Dammit, take them anyhow.* If I went to the trouble to get 'em the least you can do is take a couple!"

Tess took the pills, but in his anger at Tess, Degar forgot all about Eliza.

After a short rest Eliza suggested that they take a ride around town to see if any fall color was left.

"Eliza, I don't feel real good," Tess said.

"I'm sorry, Tess. I bet a little ride will make you feel better."

They got into the car with Tess in the back seat. As they drove down Beach Road Tess suddenly had violent cramps and was nauseated. She cried out and seemed to develop some spasms. Eliza reached back to comfort her.

"Degar, I'm afraid Tess is bad off. I think she needs a doctor."

"Now where in the hell I'm gonna find a doctor on Thanksgiving afternoon? You know none of 'em will be in their office on a holiday!"

"What about the doctor you told me about when I didn't feel good awhile back? He was so nice. I bet he'd help Tess. His name was Jones."

"That's right, Doctor Evan Jones. Well, we can drive by his house and see. She probably just ate too much."

Somewhat reluctantly Degar drove to the north side of town and found the doctor's house. When Doctor Evans was told that Tess was doubled up with pain he came quickly out to the car and examined her.

"She's in an extreme condition and I can't treat her here. She needs to go to the hospital. I'll call over there and ask the doctor on duty to see her. You need to hurry because she really needs some help."

They proceeded to the hospital and the attending physician, Dr. Frank Champion, felt that the situation was critical. He recommended pumping out her stomach immediately. Afterwards he gave her an elixir to settle her stomach and insisted that she spend the night in the hospital.

"She probably just ate too much Thanksgiving dinner. I gave her some bicarbonate of soda tablets that the doctor at the railroad dispensary gave me. They really didn't help her none. Surely she can go home now. She seems so much better."

"Well no, Mr. Loghin, she's had a pretty bad time and I think we need to watch her. I want her to stay at least overnight. Call us in the morning."

Tess had a restless night, not so much from her illness, but because she was fretting about going dancing with Jake on Friday. Degar didn't call all night, he just appeared at the hospital rather early the next morning.

"I came to pick up my daughter, Tess Loghin. Is she ready to go?"

"The doctor left instructions that if her breakfast didn't upset her she could go home. She ate about an hour ago. It seems she's doing all right now, so she can leave."

"Now I'm taking you straight home and I'm telling you that you've gotta stay there. There'll be no dancing for you tonight, young lady," Degar declared on the way home.

"But Papa, I feel all right now."

"I don't care how you feel now, you ain't going and that's that!"

Once home—and after Eliza quit fussing over her—Tess called Jake. "Jake, I hate to tell you this but I can't go dancing tonight."

"Why Tess, what's wrong?"

"I've just gotten home from the hospital and—"

"The hospital? What in the world happened? Why were you there?"

"Papa said I ate too much Thanksgiving dinner. The doctor seemed to think I had some sort of food poisoning. Golly, I was really sick. They pumped my stomach out and kept me overnight to be sure I was all right. I'm feeling fine now."

"If you're fine now why can't you go?"

"I'm so sorry, so very sorry, but Papa won't let me. I guess he thinks I need to rest."

"I'm sorry too, Tess. Maybe we can do it next week."

"I'd like that."

But the next week Tess continued to be sickly and did not attend school at all. Evelyn's mother became very concerned and decided to notify Tess' grandmother in South Carolina. Her grandmother, Mary Mann, called and offered to come up and help, but Degar declined the offer. He explained that a similar incident had happened before and assured her that Tess would be all right and that Eliza was taking good care of her.

The following Monday, Tess stayed home and her condition continued to worsen. Fairly early, Eliza answered a knock at the door and saw a little lady standing there.

"I'm Mary Mann, and I understand that my granddaughter is sick. I would like to see her."

"Hello, Mrs. Mann. I'm Eliza Harper. Degar told me that you might come up, but there's no reason for you to feel you have to be here. We're doing the best we can for her."

"Well maybe so, but I still need to see her."

Since she was so insistent Eliza stepped back and let Mrs. Mann enter the house. She found Tess in the bedroom sweating profusely and apparently suffering a great deal. Mary tried to comfort her, but to no avail.

"She's been having these spells now and then but she gets over them," Eliza told her.

Tess looked up at her grandmother and attempted a smile, but could only whisper a few words of love. Suddenly, she cried out in pain, and extended and clenched her hands and feet. Her shuddering and convulsions increased so much that Eliza and Mary decided to call Degar at the shop. When they reached him he called a doctor.

As the pain racked her body Tess began to wonder if she would ever see her friends again—particularly Jake. She thought fleetingly of the fun she'd had at school, the picnics, the dancing. In the whirling, heated reverie, a red blankness enveloped her brain and then the pain was suddenly gone. She thought of Jake and imagined her mother in heaven, and in that last pleasantness a small, unrequited portion of love silently returned to the infinite and eternal source of all love.

Dr. Williams arrived at the Loghin's house, checked her vital signs, and gave her an injection in an attempt to stimulate her heart.

"I'm so sorry, but she's dead. There's nothing else that can be done. I called an ambulance before I left my office. It should be here in any minute." When the driver and attendant came to the door Dr. Williams asked them to take Tess' body to the hospital. "I was told that she had a similar incident about a week ago and that she was taken to the hospital. I thought that the doctor who treated her there should be advised, and possibly examine the body if he feels so inclined," Williams said.

When they reached the hospital a nurse led Eliza and Mary to the waiting room, explaining that only doctors and nurses were allowed into the emergency room proper. In the emergency room Dr. Jenner Hughes pulled back the blanket covering the body on the gurney and saw a young girl dressed in a frayed cotton night-gown. The nurse, Rosa Turner, checked the pulse and Dr. Hughes listened for a heartbeat.

"I don't get a heartbeat. No heartbeat at all," he told Nurse Turner.

"There's no sign of a pulse that I can find, but she's still a little warm."

"Well if she's dead, I don't know why they brought her here.

There's absolutely nothing we can do for her." He pulled a sheet over Tess' body, removed a yellow tag from a drawer, and tied it onto her big toe. He printed her name on the tag, along with "D.O.A."

"Apparently Dr. Williams was called to her house, and when he got there the housekeeper and grandmother were with the girl. He found no signs of life when he examined her. Since he never had a chance to treat her he thought he should send her over here. The housekeeper told him that the girl had been to the hospital on Thanksgiving, so Dr. Williams thought the doctor who'd treated her at that time might want to examine her," Nurse Turner explained.

"We need her records to identify her first doctor. We'll have to contact the Records department."

At about that time Degar burst into the room, despite attempts to hold him back. He was dressed in a beaked cap and grease-spattered coveralls.

"I was called and told that my daughter, Tess Loghin, was being brought here. I'm her father and I want to know her condition."

"I'm sorry, but your daughter was dead before she arrived."

"Oh my god, you mean that my little Tess is dead? Can't you do something for her?" he exclaimed.

"I'm sorry. There's nothing we can do now."

"I love her so much," Degar replied, going over, removing the sheet from her head, kissing her on the forehead, and sobbing. He left the room and joined Eliza and Mary, who were both crying.

Degar returned to the room when the record of the Thanksgiving visit was brought in.

"It seems she was treated by Dr. William Champion that day, but was released the next day, last Friday. I see that some stuff was sent to the pathology department, but there's no pathology report in here," said Dr. Hughes. They paged Dr. Champion, who happened to be in the hospital visiting his patients.

"I treated her for what I diagnosed as severe stomach pain caused by overeating on Thanksgiving. I pumped her stomach and sent the contents to pathology, but when I called them the next morning no pathology had been performed. Since I discharged her that day, they were probably discarded. She seemed quite normal when she left Friday," Champion explained.

Degar joined the conversation. "And she was quite normal this morning when I left early for work. All I left out for her to take were some bicarbonate of soda tablets."

"We'll need to examine that container and any of the tablets that remain."

"I'll be sure to get them for you." With that Degar left the room, tears still streaming down his face. He asked a desk attendant for directions to a pay phone and made a short call. Afterwards he returned to Eliza and Mary in the waiting room.

"There's an undertaker here with the 'meat wagon'," an ambulance driver announced to the doctors in the emergency room.

"Well we can't keep the body here unless there's to be an autopsy."

Rosa called Degar into the room and sat him down. "Do you want to have an autopsy?" she asked.

"I will not let my precious Tess be all cut up for an autopsy! I want to bury her in South Carolina where my mother is buried."

"Well since it looks like she died of natural causes, and we

90

can't have an autopsy unless we have your consent, we'll go ahead and take her body to the mortuary."

They placed Tess' body on a gurney and into the undertaker's van. After speaking with Dr. Champion for a few more minutes Degar and the women left.

"It's too bad that such a young girl died. I thought it was rather unusual that her little hands were clenched, almost like rigor mortis had set in," said Nurse Turner.

Dr. Hughes thought for a moment. "I didn't really notice that, but she was somewhat warm so it couldn't be rigor. I noticed that her feet were sort of stiff when I tagged her toe, though. We'll have to leave it to the doctors involved."

Rosa continued to speculate. "I wonder why she died? It could have been suicide—so many people are depressed because of the hard times. It could have been something brought on by malnourishment. She was mighty thin. I guess we will never know."

Later that night the undertaker, Mr. Woolvin, called Degar at home.

"Mr. Loghin, I'll need a death certificate before I can prepare the body for burial."

"A death certificate! Well where do I get one from?"

"From her doctor. He should give you one."

Degar called Dr. Williams and requested a death certificate, but Williams wouldn't sign it because Tess had died before he arrived at the Loghin's house. He also expressed some uncertainty about the cause of death. Degar called Dr. Champion, but he also refused to sign the death certificate because he didn't attend her at the time of her death.

This caused quite a dilemma—no death certificate, no burial. So nothing was done. Later, Degar asked Mr. Woolvin for help, certain that this sort of situation had happened before. Finally, Woolvin agreed to take care of it.

The undertaker called Dr. Champion who, after a lengthy discussion, agreed to sign. He listed the cause of death as "idiopathic convulsions," which he said was the reason for her treatment the week before. The body was then taken to Woolvin's morgue, embalmed, and, upon instructions from Degar, placed in a small cheap coffin and prepared for burial in the cemetery where Degar's mother was buried in South Carolina. The casket left on the southbound train the next night and Degar accompanied it to the burial spot. He stood by as Tess was lowered into the grave. At the service the local Baptist minister consoled those present by explaining that there was "A time for all seasons. A time to live and a time to die." He questioned why so many sinless youth die so young and why many evil people live long and sinful lives. Because of her motherless youth and her love for her father, he assured them all that Tess was now entering the kingdom of heaven.

Back in Wilmington, Jake missed seeing Tess at school; he had no information about her death since there was no obituary in the local paper. He tried to call her home, but received no

92

answer. He heard of Tess' death with the rest of his class, when the homeroom teacher, Miss Montgomery, read a notice that Tess Loghin had died after a short illness.

"It's a shame that a youth, so bright and shining and full of love, hope, and potential has passed from the world. Please students, stand for a moment and say a silent prayer for Tess and for her father who will miss her, as we all will."

After school Jake went home and told Carrie. "Tess is dead! Isn't that just awful Carrie? She was a sweet friend. I can't believe it."

"Lawd, chile, you mean that young'n done pass't away?"

"Yeah, she died. I believe that her daddy did it. She always told me that he scared her—even beat her. She was such a nice person and he was so mean to her," Jake said through his tears.

"Don't you cry, Jake, she's with Jesus. You know de 'postle John say in de Bible dat de Lord has many houses for folks in heaven. Surely dat chile will find a good one with her mother, who you say went on many years ago. There is a time to live and a time to die, and remember dat time will come to all of us whether we is good or bad," Carrie said.

"I hope her daddy goes to hell," Jake said.

"Now honey, don't you say things like that. He is prob'ly as sad as you. You've lost a friend but he'z lost a daughter. Let me fix you a little som'em to eat. Maybe it'll make you feel better."

"Thanks just the same but I'm not hungry. I think I'll go walk over by the lake; I need to think a little bit."

Later when Jake's mother came home they sat down to talk.

"Jake, it's hard to understand death at times, especially in one so young," Sarah Jones said. "It doesn't seem fair, does it? But remember you'll always have memories of your friendship with

Tess. In a way she'll live on in you. When you're older you'll be able to understand that death is a part of life and you'll be able to accept that fact easier then."

Although Jake found some comfort in Carrie's and his mother's words, he was still puzzled that a sweet girl like Tess could die so young. His confusion was compounded because he remembered the awful treatment she received at the hands of her father. It all seemed so unfair. Deep inside he felt a certain amount of responsibility. Tess had shared her feelings about Degar, had told Jake about her fears. He hadn't known how to help her. He did nothing.

Part II

1936-1937

Chapter Thirteen

Dennis Coleman awoke in the morning still tired from the previous day's work. He had gotten home around eleven o'clock the night before after attending a stakeout aimed at some bootleggers suspected of landing a load of illicit booze on the Sound near the rail trestle. They didn't show, and Dennis came home to find Emma, his new wife, waiting for him. The double-bed calisthenics that followed were lively and gratifying to his tired body, and even though it added to his weariness, he enthusiastically participated. He glanced at the clock, carefully crawled over Emma, and eased out of bed. Emma had been his high school sweetheart and they had wanted to get married for some time. Financial considerations had delayed their union. He dressed quietly and opened the door to the bedroom.

"You were up mighty late last night, but it didn't seem to slow you down," Emma said quietly.

"Yeah, Adam had a pretty good idea when he gave up that rib."

"I agree." With that he closed the door and left.

Dennis was a deputy at the county sheriff's department where he had worked for about ten years. These days he was in charge of criminal investigations. He was thirty years old, dark-haired, and wore a permanent smile on his face. He had finished high school, gone to a sheriff's training school, and was now considered a valuable asset to the department.

When he entered the boarding house nearby to get breakfast, the owner called out a welcome. "Glad you're here. Haven't seen you since you got married. Won't Emma cook you any breakfast? I'm glad you finally married her, you all had messed around long enough. But I must say, I miss seeing her with you at breakfast."

Dennis grunted, but made no response. He sat down at the big breakfast table and put away a strong cup of coffee, some grits, and ham and eggs before he headed to the sheriff's office.

Sheriff Dawkins greeted him when he came in. "Dennis, I've been looking for you. There's a lady here who's been raising hell about her son-in-law, accusing him of murdering her daughter and granddaughter. I believe it's probably a typical jealous rage against a son-in-law, but I want you to talk to her and look into it."

Dennis entered the small conference room where he found a slight, greying lady sitting patiently. She introduced herself as Mrs. Bailey Mann.

"My daughter, Grace Mann, was married to Degar Loghin and she died in 1922 just after my granddaughter Tess Loghin was born. I came up with my husband to see Grace just before she died and we found her suffering great pain. She mumbled something about being poisoned, and at the time her husband Degar agreed— food poisoning he said. She died that afternoon, crying out in great pain, with her limbs extended and her hands clenched."

"Lady, that happened years ago. You don't expect us to go back that far and look into it, do you? We've got too many things going on here right now."

"No, but last week someone here in Wilmington called and told me that my granddaughter, Tess, was very sick. I came up and found her in bed suffering in the same way, with her daddy's housekeeper attending her. No one called the doctor until I came. When the doctor finally got there she was already dead, but she appeared in the same condition as my daughter had all those years ago. I believe that Degar arranged both of their deaths. His second wife, Ginny, died some months ago, and I've heard that she suffered the same way."

Dennis was taken aback by Mrs. Mann's story. "I'll talk to the Sheriff, and if he agrees we'll take it up with the district attorney and get authorization for an investigation. In the meantime leave your name, address, and telephone number where I can reach you, and we'll be in touch with you." He ushered her out with a few words of condolence. Later that morning Dennis met with Sheriff Dawkins.

"It's probably another one of those family suspicions that will lead to nothing, but we need to check it out. In the meantime go out to Loghin's house on Beach Road and look around. Talk to the neighbors and let me hear from you," Dawkins said.

Sheriff Dawkins arranged a meeting with the district attorney, William Odom, that afternoon.

"It could be a heinous case of first-degree murder. Poison cases are the most blatant cases of 'lying in wait' to kill someone. We'll need Grace Mann's and Tess Loghin's death certificates. We'll also need to check all the pharmacies in the area to see if Loghin purchased any poisonous substances," Odom said after Dawkins had finished sharing the facts he'd gathered thus far.

Dennis was tired but decided that he would go out to Beach

Road and take a look at the Loghin's house. It was fairly well kept with a fence around the yard. A neighbor came out and motioned Dennis over.

"I'm the mother of one of Tess' friends. I hope you're looking into Tess' death. Strange things have been going on around there. I knew she was real sick and his wife Ginny died about three months ago. Tess asked me to call her grandmother to come up here, and she did. He buried them both real quick, and after Ginny died, almost before you knew it, another lady moved in. She's in there now."

"Who is she?"

"I don't know her full name, but I've heard him call her Eliza. She told me she came here a month or so ago from Cincinnati. She seems pretty nice to me, but she's certainly not as nice as Ginny. I wish they would both leave."

"Tess Loghin's grandmother told us about her death and Mrs. Mann was here when Tess died."

"Yeah, I was the one who notified her that Tess wasn't doing well."

Dennis walked toward the back yard and looked over the fence. He saw the usual accumulation of junk, but nothing significant.

"Loghin kept an old hound dog back there, but it died a few months back. I saw Tess and a boy in the neighborhood take it across the road. Tess told me later that they buried it there."

Dennis could see a lady inside the Loghin house and decided to go no farther. After he left he rode around the neighborhood. At the big house on the next corner he saw a young teenager climbing into an old tree house. He stopped and asked the boy's name. It was Jake Jones. Dennis asked if he had known Tess.

"Sure. I not only knew her, we were good friends. We were in the same grade at school together. I figure that her father did something to her. She told me that she was afraid of him and thought he would really harm her some day. I think he may have killed his dog too, because Tess told me that it got sick suddenly and died one night. She got me to help her bury it, and we took it across the road, dug a hole, and put it inside; I guess it's still there."

Dennis returned to the station and called to see if the record office had sent over the death certificates. After a short pause the clerk came back on the line.

"The Grace Mann certificate from 1922 is here, showing death by heart attack. Tess and Ginny Loghin's certificates have been delayed for some reason. I can't seem to find them. I don't understand it unless someone has removed them."

"Well please look for them, and if you get any information give me a call at the Sheriff's office." In the meantime, Coleman decided to see what he could find out about Degar Loghin.

At about four o'clock in the afternoon he went to the north side of town and parked near the roundhouse where he saw some of the railroad men leaving. He asked a nearby man if he knew Loghin and was directed to a rather gaunt and thin man who was getting into a car. He followed the car as it parked near the North Side Bar 'N Grill. He entered the grill shortly after Degar and ordered a beer. A man came in close to five o'clock and joined Degar.

Dennis asked the waitress who the second man was and she said his name was Jere something. Dennis moved over a little closer where he could hear their conversation. Jere was lamenting the death of Degar's daughter. He heard Degar thank Jere, and the conversation turned to the topic of life insurance; he couldn't make out the gist of it, but it remained in the back of his mind. Degar and Jere left about ten minutes later.

"I hope some day we can go on another trip like we did last May when we went to Cincinnati to help clean up that train wreck," Degar said as they were leaving.

"Yeah, I hope so too, but I believe you had a better time than I did." Degar's only response was a laugh.

At the office the next morning Dennis conferred with Sheriff Dawkins and shared the small bits of information he had been able to pick up.

"Dennis, there are several things I want you to do: Go talk to the doctors who signed the death certificates; check with the local life insurance offices about insurance on Tess; find out more about Degar's friends and neighbors; and follow up with the pharmacies in town to see if Degar made any unusual purchases."

Dennis was excited to be in charge of the investigation. He had a hunch that there was something wrong at the Loghin house—based largely on the determined manner in which Mary Mann presented her suspicions and on his conversation with Jake and the neighbor.

Dennis decided to try the pharmacies first. The main ones were on Front Street, but after visiting all three he found no evidence that Degar had ever purchased anything from them. The others were also a bust. But then the druggist at a small store on Ninth Street told him about an inquiry several months back about the purchase of strychnine for use in protecting property from roaming dogs.

"He was a gaunt-looking man with dark features, a laboring

type, wearing a hat. I don't know his name. He wasn't a regular customer. I don't think he lived in the neighborhood."

When Dennis returned to the office he looked around and found a book about poisons. It stated that strychnine, when mixed in small amounts with other ingredients, could be used as a therapeutic medicine for a tonic. Strychnine was deadly if used in excess of a therapeutic dose—about two milligrams or less.

He couldn't understand why someone would use this method. It could easily be discovered in the body and would certainly turn up if an autopsy had been performed. The next day inquires at the hospital confirmed that no autopsies had taken place.

Chapter Fourteen

The next morning, Dennis was up early and went to Dr. Victor Williams' office. Williams was the doctor Eliza and Mary Mann had called the day Tess died, but he had gotten there too late. He was also the one who had refused to sign the death certificate.

When he entered the doctor's office, Dennis found Williams quite willing to talk about the case.

"I understand you went by Tess Loghin's house the day she died?" Dennis said.

"Yes, they called me. I went over there immediately. I checked for vital signs, detected no heartbeat, and she wasn't breathing."

"Had you ever treated her before?"

"No, I had never treated anyone in the family before, but when I was called in for the emergency, I felt that I had to respond. When I arrived I could tell that the girl had suffered severely before death, and I considered it serious enough to have a question as to whether the death was due to natural causes."

"Could it have been poison?" Dennis asked.

"I'm not sure, but I wouldn't sign the death certificate because there had been no autopsy and I had no history of the patient to go on. I understand that she had been in the hospital recently and that her stomach had been pumped, but those records were not available to me. I don't know whether any pathology was done on the contents of her stomach, either at that time, or when she was brought in after I saw her."

"Dr. Champion signed the death certificate finally, with the cause stated as 'idiopathic convulsions.' Do you know what that means?"

"No, you'll have to ask him. He treated her the first time, and I understand the symptoms were similar."

Dennis left the office more confused than ever, and when he reported to Sheriff Dawkins, he was directed to contact Dr. Champion to discuss the case with him. Dennis also thought it was funny that the dog had died in June—shortly after Jere and Degar had returned from the trip to Cincinnati. Degar's second wife died sometime thereafter; this raised a suspicion that the poison, if it existed, could have been purchased out of town. He recalled Jake's statement that Tess thought the dog may have been poisoned.

"Sheriff, do we need to get a permit to dig up a dog that's buried across the road from the Loghin house?" Dennis asked. "I talked to the young boy who helped Loghin's daughter bury the dog, and I believe we can find it. It's only been about six or seven months."

" I don't believe so, but I'll check with the district attorney and let you know."

The next morning Dennis got approval to disinter the dog.

Had it been buried on the Loghin's property they would have needed a search warrant and they didn't have enough evidence to apply for one yet.

Dennis realized that Jake Jones was the son of the local lawyer Caleb Jones, and he didn't feel he could talk to the boy again without telling Caleb about the situation.

"Dennis, what in the world do you want with me? All my clients are either in jail or on the run, and I surely don't have any here in the office for you to arrest!" Caleb cried as Dennis entered his office.

"It's about the death of a girl, Tess Loghin, who lived down the road from you and went to school with your son Jake. Jake mentioned that he helped her bury her dog. We have some suspicion that the dog was poisoned and may want to dig it up to see if there is any poison residue. I didn't want to ask him to help me without your permission, and I want to make sure that this is all done in confidence."

"I'll talk to him tonight and call you tomorrow. He's been upset over Tess' death, and I'm sure he'll keep it in confidence and try to help. I'll want him to have protection."

"We'll certainly give him that."

When Caleb returned home that evening, he told Jake about his meeting with Dennis.

"Yeah, Dad, that's the deputy who talked to me. I told him about burying the dog, and that Tess thought her dad had killed it."

"Will you go with him and show him where you and Tess buried the dog?"

"Yes, I'll be glad to. Tess was very afraid of her father. He mistreated her all the time."

Dennis received this news the next day and arranged to meet Jake that afternoon at his house. He, Jake, and two men with shovels crossed the road and walked south through the woods to a point about fifty yards across from the Loghin house. The woods were covered with fallen leaves, but after raking around for a while they found the remains of the small cross Tess had placed there. A short dig uncovered the burlap bag covered with maggots. Although the stench was unpleasant, the bag was removed and placed in a sealed box that Dennis had brought with him.

"Jake, I told your dad that all of this must be kept quiet. You're not to tell anyone about what we've done."

"Yeah, he told me, and I would hate for Tess' dad to know about it. You can count on me."

Jake left thinking that it would be ironic if Sis became the key to finding the cause of the Tess' death.

When Dennis returned to the courthouse, Sheriff Dawkins greeted him with news about the autopsy.

"I've been calling around to see who in the world can do an autopsy on a dog. There's no veterinary hospital in this state, so we're going to have to send the remains to Georgia to get a report. I've made the arrangements, and we'll send it off on the afternoon train to Atlanta."

Dennis left, puzzled over the entire situation. If the dog was poisoned they would still have to prove that Degar bought the poison and that Tess and her stepmother had been poisoned, but it would probably be too farfetched to go back to 1922 and dig up Grace Mann. The most they could hope for was for Tess and Ginny to be disinterred and some residue of the poison to be found in their bodies. He also thought of the conversation he had heard between Degar and Jere Swain about a trip on the railroad shortly before the dog died, and before Ginny Loghin died. What about the mysterious lady who had moved in after Ginny's death? Could she be a key to the poison purchase? It would be an almost impossible task to check the pharmacies that far away, but it might be their only hope. Dennis decided to wait on the dog's autopsy. He also considered getting a picture of Degar to show to the pharmacist on Ninth Street who had had the inquiry about strychnine. Maybe he could identify Loghin.

Dennis was instructed to check at the life insurance offices to see if there was any insurance on Ginny or Tess Loghin. He began checking the local offices and finally found that Loghin had collected on *two* policies on Tess, one with Metropolitan Life Insurance Company and another with a different company shortly after her death. A strange thing about the Met policy was that Degar had paid the premium four weeks in advance in November. He had never paid in advance before. Since Tess died on December 1, Degar had received a small return premium in addition to the approximate $1,000 he had received from the policies at her death. He had also collected payments on polices for Ginny Loghin and his first wife, Grace Mann. Dennis made notes of this and reported it to District Attorney Odom and Sheriff Dawkins the next day.

"This must have been the motive, if he killed them, but it may be hard to make a jury believe that a person would kill for such a small amount," Dawkins speculated.

"But he had apparently brought in a new girlfriend who came down from up north, and she could have been making demands on him that he couldn't handle. Since we don't have any evidence that he did them in, we don't know," Odom replied.

The meeting ended with instructions for Dennis to make further inquiries.

Chapter Fifteen

The next morning Dennis went to Dr. William Champion's office, and after he sat in the waiting room for about an hour, the nurse came out.

"Dr. Champion will see you now for about fifteen minutes. He has to go to the hospital to check on his patients soon."

"What can I help you with, son?" Dr. Champion asked when Dennis went in.

"I'm with the sheriff's department, and we're looking into circumstances surrounding the death of Tess Loghin. The death certificate shows that you treated her."

"Yes, I treated her sometime around Thanksgiving when they brought her in with terrible stomach cramps. I thought the cause of it was too much Thanksgiving dinner, but she was in such pain that I had her stomach pumped and gave her some medicine. She appeared better after that, and I released her."

"Did you see her again before she died?"

"No."

"Did you analyze the contents of her stomach on Thanksgiving?"

"No, she was a charity patient, and since it was a holiday, I would have had to call in the pathology department. I didn't want the hospital to bear that expense. Since she recovered so quickly I didn't think it was necessary."

"How did you happen to sign the death certificate?"

"Well, I understand that Dr. Williams saw her shortly after she died. He wouldn't sign it because he hadn't treated her. The undertaker called me and said that it was a formality needed before she could be embalmed and buried. He told me that she had symptoms similar to those that had appeared when I treated her a few days earlier. I assumed that her problems had returned, and I signed the death certificate giving 'idiopathic convulsions' as the probable cause of her death."

"What do you mean by that?"

"It can mean a lot of things, but mostly it means that the body has been infected by something which is affecting the brain and the body, causing convulsions that are usually uncontrollable. It can also come as a type of epilepsy, and I felt that there were symptoms of this at the time of my treatment. I assumed they returned in a more severe form. Convulsions can be caused by several diseases, but without expensive research and tests it can't be determined with any certainty."

"Then you don't know exactly what killed her?"

"No, but she suffered convulsions just before she died, and the undertaker told me that her limbs were stiff, and her hands and feet extended and clenched. This could have been caused by a number of diseases."

"Would a dose of poison cause this?"

"I'm not familiar with the effects of poison on the body, but I

111

assume there are some poisons that result in a painful death and some that would result in a very benign death. No one ever said that poison was a possibility, so no check was made for it. Now, I'm sorry but I must go!" With that the doctor picked up his hat and left in a hurry.

Dennis was more confused than ever by the offhanded manner in which the death certificate was signed, but made notes so he could report later.

Later in the day he called Dr. Williams again to share what he had learned. In response to the question regarding poison Williams said that it was a possibility, that some poisons could cause convulsions. He confirmed that expensive tests would be needed to make a final determination.

Dennis called Dr. Cowan's office, the physician who had signed Ginny Loghin's death certificate, and made an appointment to speak to him the next day. Cowan was very cooperative.

"I had treated Mrs. Loghin in early June for a gynecological condition and for complaints regarding her stomach. I gave her an injection at that time and she recovered, and I didn't hear any more from her until the first week in July. At that time I was called to her house for an emergency. I got to the house in about thirty minutes, but she was taken to the hospital. She died shortly after arrival. At the time I examined her I concluded that she'd had a heart attack. I remember noting that her limbs were extended and that her hands were clenched. I concluded that this was caused by the pain of the sudden heart attack."

"Did you discuss this with Dr. Williams after you were told of Tess Loghin's death?"

"Yes, I did. He told me you questioned him yesterday

afternoon. As a result of our conference, we both concluded that the deaths had been very similar—particularly with respect to the pain preceding them and the condition of the limbs and hands before rigor mortis set in."

"Did you discuss the possibility of poisoning?"

"He said you had mentioned it, but he wasn't familiar with the symptoms, and I wouldn't know much about it either. We're having a staff meeting day after tomorrow, and I'm going to bring this up so that we can discuss it."

Dennis left, and to further his investigation, he went to the dispensary at the basement of the railroad headquarters. After some inquiry he learned that Degar Loghin had in fact obtained bicarbonate of soda pills and other nonprescription stomach cures throughout the last summer and fall.

The next night, Dennis received a call from Sheriff Dawkins. A telegram had come in from the laboratory in Georgia. There was evidence of strychnine shown in the Loghin's dog's remains. A full report was on its way to Wilmington. Dawkins suggested that they meet with the District Attorney Odom in the morning so that Dennis could give a full report.

Chapter Sixteen

Dennis arrived at the office at 8:30 the next morning to find Sheriff Dawkins waiting for him. They walked across the street to the district attorney's small office. The caption on the door said "William Odom, Attorney at Law." Even though Odom was allowed to practice as a private lawyer, he held a public office and received a small salary from the meager county budget for his work.

Bill Odom was a big, heavyset man with dark features and a booming voice, which when directed towards a jury, could be heard through the windows a block from the courthouse. When Dennis and Dawkins came in he was enjoying his favorite brand of tobacco, Indian Chew. He spit in the nearby spittoon and cleared his throat. "Good morning, Joe, I guess you're here about the Loghin case."

"Yes, Bill, and I brought Dennis Coleman with me so he could give you the results of his investigation so far. Go ahead Dennis."

"First, I've been all over town to the pharmacies and have found no evidence of poison purchased by Loghin. We dug up his dog that died last June, and there was evidence of strychnine in the remains, although the amount was not estimated. This indicates that there had been poison on the premises. Loghin was living with a woman who had apparently moved in shortly after his wife Ginny died under circumstances similar to his daughter. The new woman apparently came to town from Ohio or West Virginia, and I understand Loghin had been there on railroad business in May.

"I've talked to all the doctors involved, and they disagree about why Mrs. Loghin's death certificate is based on 'heart attack' and Tess' on 'idiopathic convulsions.' I asked Dr. Champion about this and his explanation was completely confusing. He said that it's a Greek word, but I don't know what that means."

"I certainly don't want to go before a local jury talking about things in Greek. We'll have to get with these doctors and try to see if there's a possibility that the ladies were poisoned. If we can't prove Loghin had poison we may be stuck," said Odom.

"Jake Jones, Caleb's son, directed us to the buried dog. Apparently he was aware of Tess' fear of her daddy, and how upset she was when Eliza Harper moved in shortly after her stepmother's death. All this happened shortly after Loghin had been in Ohio to help clear up a train wreck. The doctors are going to have a staff meeting tomorrow and the deaths will be discussed."

"Dennis, call Dr. Williams and see when the staff meeting will be held and tell him that I'd like to come and talk with them about it. Go down to the railroad and talk to my friend Bill David in the Legal department to see when this trip was taken. I would be afraid to have you talk to Jere Swain; we don't want to arouse suspicion. I understand he and Loghin are good friends.

Chances are he may have been smart enough to purchase strychnine in Ohio so there would be no record here, but I don't believe I can prove a case just on the dog without exhuming the women's bodies. I doubt that I could get an order right now," said Odom.

Sheriff Dawkins agreed to go to the railroad, and Dennis would call and make arrangements for Odom to meet with the doctors.

After a telephone call to the railroad's Legal department Dawkins arrived at Bill David's office in the afternoon.

"Hi, Joe, glad to see you. You know that we here at the railroad are always ready, willing, and able to cooperate with the local law enforcement people."

"I'm here because we're investigating the death of the daughter of a man named Degar Loghin who works in the shops. We understand that he went to Ohio to help with the cleanup of a wreck."

"Do you know approximately when the wreck happened?" David asked.

"Yes, it happened on the night of May tenth. The contingent from here, including Loghin, went up on the eleventh, and returned here on the sixteenth. They spent four nights in Cincinnati and about three days traveling."

"Can you tell where they stayed?"

"I was hoping you'd check your records for me."

David made a call and issued instructions to find the record of the trip. Shortly thereafter a secretary came in with a stack of records from which David extracted a hotel bill.

"The records show that they stayed in the York Hotel, which

116

is near the railroad station near the business district."

"Can you give me a number so that I can call the hotel and see if there are drugstores nearby?" Dawkins asked.

"Sure, here it is on this bill."

"You know we're investigating circumstances surrounding suspicious deaths. It's important to keep this confidential."

"Certainly. We'll respect your request and be ready to help at any time. I understand that you'll be up for reelection in the spring, so let me know if I can be of help. I know you're doing a good job." With that compliment from David, Dawkins left.

Later he called the York Hotel and verified the date of Swain and Loghin's stay. The clerk also told him that there were two drugstores within two blocks of the hotel.

The next day District Attorney Odom went to the hospital and was directed to a conference room where the doctors had already gathered. They knew why he was there, but seemed to show no embarrassment about the confusion over the two death certificates.

Odom opened with a blast. "What in the world do you mean by putting on a death certificate 'idiopathic convulsions' and saying it could be caused by a number of things? When someone dies don't you feel responsible to determine exactly the cause?"

"This is a medical term in the form of a question mark. 'Idiopathic' comes from two Greek words meaning 'own diseases'," Dr. Champion explained.

"So you don't really know the cause of Tess' death?"

"No, because the convulsions could have been caused by several diseases."

Dr. Williams spoke up. "I didn't sign the certificate because I didn't treat the girl. I arrived shortly after she died. But the manner of her death was strange and extreme, and the way her hands were clenched and her body was extended, I felt she had died in great pain. I talked to Dr. Cowan, who treated Ginny Loghin, and the deaths were so similar that I thought something was probably wrong. Since I didn't treat either of them I went no further."

Odom began to question the group. "Didn't any of you have enough medical curiosity to think that either or both of these two ladies had received some kind of poison? Please discuss it and see if your medical books can give you any information on the effect of strychnine on the body of a person who has received a lethal dose."

After he left, there were many questions in his mind about the medical information. When he returned to his office he called Dawkins. After a rather long conversation he said, "Joe, I believe that we'll have to send Dennis to Cincinnati to check those drug-stores—even though it will strain our budget to do it. We could call the drugstores, but I doubt if we could get much useful information by telephone, and we don't know which store it was."

"I'll talk to Dennis and see what we can arrange. The sheriff's department can get passes on the railroad for official business," Dawkins replied.

That afternoon Dennis went back out on Beach Road to the Loghin house to see if there were any changes there. He wanted to speak to Eliza Harper. When he parked, the neighbor he had talked to previously came running out to his car.

"Last night Eliza Harper came over to the house and told me that she was leaving to go back home to Ohio. She left me an address where she could be reached. I can give it to you if you want it. I think she took the morning train out of here."

"Did she tell you why she was leaving?"

"No, but she seemed rather upset, and maybe a little fearful."

"Will you be kind enough to get that address for me?"

"Yes, it's in the house. It won't be any problem, I know exactly where it is. I'll just go and get it for you now."

She returned shortly with the piece of paper Eliza had given her and gave it to Dennis. He thanked her, got in his car, and started to drive off. Just as he was leaving, he looked back and saw Degar drive into the yard and go into his house. Dennis slowed down and noticed that Degar came right back out with a paper in his hand. It was as if he were looking for something or someone.

Dennis called Dawkins and reported these rather unusual circumstances to him.

"Well, she probably got wind of our investigation, became a little scared living there when people were getting suspicious. I bet that Loghin found her in Ohio when he was up there and promised her a beautiful life if she came back and lived with him. I doubt he described the possible risk," Dawkins said.

Dawkins called Bill Odom at home and told him what had happened. Odom asked him to call the railroad and make arrangements for Dennis to go to Cincinnati to check out the drugstores and to interview Eliza Harper.

Chapter Seventeen

Early the next day Sheriff Dawkins went to the county finance office where he found the treasurer seated at his desk drinking coffee.

"Hi, Sheriff. What brings you here so early?"

"Well, we're trying to solve a problem about the death of a young girl here, and it looks like it will be necessary to send a deputy to Ohio."

"The travel budget is under a lot of pressure right now. What do you estimate it will cost?"

"About $300."

"Let me see, I think we have a little in the reserve account."

"We really need it. This is a serious murder case, and we want to handle it before any publicity breaks."

"I see here that we can handle it, and if there's a hurry you can pick it up this afternoon," the treasurer said after some thought.

Later Dawkins called the railroad and arranged for a pass for Dennis and Emma. He felt that the young married couple would enjoy a little time together on the trip, and that Emma might even be of some help in interviewing Eliza Harper. He also knew that

Dennis would really appreciate it; he'd had no time off since his wedding. Although he received a family pass, Dawkins was only able to get it for one lower Pullman berth. He chuckled to himself over this.

"I've arranged a trip for you to go on Wednesday and return on Monday, so you'll have two days and the weekend to try to talk to Eliza Harper, and to find a drugstore that sold poison to Degar," Dawkins said when Dennis came in.

"That sounds good to me. I think I can do it and maybe get some answers."

"Also, I thought you might like it if Emma could go with you. You two may have some fun over the weekend."

"Thanks a lot. I'll talk to her. If she's agreeable, and I'm sure she will be, we'll be ready in plenty of time."

Emma was more than agreeable. "I can't wait! We didn't get to take a honeymoon trip. Since you were called in on this case I haven't seen much of you."

On the day of departure they packed their suitcases, and at about three o'clock Sheriff Dawkins drove them to the station. He walked with them through the concourse, to the Pullman car attached to the end of the train. The conductor checked the tickets, and as they boarded, the Pullman porter welcomed them.

"Come on aboard. I see you're assigned to Lower 7, and it's right here. I'll stick your bags in the berth and you can go sit in the lounge until the train leaves in about ten minutes. My name is Royce. If you need anything just let me know. I'll make your berth up at about eight o'clock so you can get plenty of rest. Dinner will be in the dining car at about six o'clock." Dennis and Emma ambled to the lounge car and found a seat.

"Well, this looks great, but I guess we'll have to flip a coin to see who gets the upper berth and who gets the lower," Emma said.

"Yeah, but they were only able to get a pass for one lower berth."

"You mean I've got to get in that little bed with you and try to sleep? I know what you'll be trying to do all night."

"I guess so, unless you want to sit up in the lounge car all night."

"Honey, it'll be you who sits up all night in the lounge car if anyone does."

"Well Emma, I guess we'll have to see how it works out."

"I doubt it will work out with me in the little berth. With the kind of acrobatics you try, we'd probably end up in the aisle—to our disgrace and the amusement of everyone on the train."

At about this time the train began to move forward through the yard and onto the north track. Soon it was in the open country, and with its resounding rhythm was passing through many small towns.

Emma and Dennis went to the dining car at about half past five. They were seated at a table with a white tablecloth and napkins and a slender vase holding a red rose. They had a splendid meal of roast beef, mashed potatoes, collard greens, and a salad, topped off with a dish of vanilla ice cream with crushed mint leaves and chocolate sauce. They were entertained by the ever-passing countryside, and by the small crowds which invariably waved to them as they passed through the stations in each town along the way.

Eventually the porter came into the lounge car. "Your berth is made up. You all can go to bed whenever you're ready," he said.

"I'm going to sleep in the berth. Mr. Coleman is afraid that if he travels in the train lying down he'll get dizzy. He's decided to sit up in the lounge car for the night," Emma told the porter.

"Well, I've got a blanket he can take up there to keep him warm, and a lot of people do that who can't get a berth. He'll be more comfortable."

With that Emma went to the Pullman berth, pulled the curtain, and hooked and buttoned it thoroughly. Dennis settled down in the lounge car with his blanket. Sometime in the night their train was switched to the C&O in Richmond, and even though Emma was lonely for Dennis she slept soundly, soothed by the clickity-clack of the wheels.

The train reached the station around one o'clock. They unloaded their bags and took a cab to the York Hotel, which was located just a short distance away. Upon registering, Dennis asked about nearby pharmacies and learned there were two several blocks away—Doctor's Drug Company and Ace Drug Company. They went to their room, and after settling down, decided to check the drugstores right away. They walked to Ace first and Dennis asked the pharmacist on duty if they kept records for sales of poisonous substances. He told them that they did.

"I'd like to look at the record for May of last year."

"I'll have to call my supervisor to get permission. It's company policy."

"It involves an investigation of a death in North Carolina. I'm with the sheriff's department there, and we believe that some sort of poison was purchased here." Dennis showed his badge and a letter from Dawkins authorizing the trip.

"I'll call my supervisor and get back to you at the hotel," the pharmacist said.

They left and went to the other store, where the clerk immediately got the record book. After perusing it Dennis thanked him and they left.

"There was one that looked suspicious to me, but I didn't want to make a big point of it. We'll wait and look at the Ace registry and later come back here to check the date of that entry. There's a similarity of names for the purchase of strychnine back on May thirteenth but I'll have to call Bill Odom and see if he thinks we can use it," he told Emma.

As they entered the hotel room the phone rang. It was the Ace pharmacist calling to say that the records could be reviewed. Dennis got in touch with Bill Odom and told him that one D. Loughlin had purchased fifty milligrams of strychnine at Doctor's Drug Company on May 13. Bill sounded like he was going to come through the phone line and hug Dennis.

"With this in an affidavit, I'm sure I can get a search warrant and the right to exhume a few bodies. I still want you to find Eliza Harper and see what she knows. I hope she'll be willing to talk and tell us why she left town," Odom said.

Dennis returned to Doctor's Drug Company and copied the following information:

May 13, 1936—Name: D. Loughlin

Address: York Hotel

Purchase: 50 mg. Strychnine

Purpose: To worm sick dog and for use in treating hogs.

Cost: $2.00 Paid: Cash

He went into Ace Drug Company and reviewed the records, but found no additional information of interest.

Emma was waiting for him at the hotel, and they were jubilant that their first few hours had been so productive. All they needed to do now was find Eliza.

They went for a walk along the Ohio River and even though it was cold, it was good to breathe the fresh Ohio air. They returned to the hotel for a good night's sleep, much more comfortable and enjoyable for Dennis than the night before.

Chapter Eighteen

When Dennis got up the next morning he was pleased with the progress he had made, but he still had the problem of locating Eliza Harper and seeing if she could shed any light on the investigation.

The address he had received from the neighbor was in a remote part of the city. A review of the telephone book revealed no Harpers listed at that address. He asked Emma if she would accompany him, explaining that Eliza might be more likely to open up if she were with him. Emma agreed.

They left the hotel and took a trolley line to a point described by the hotel clerk as being near the location. Within a few blocks they found the address. The house was a small bungalow in fairly good repair, with many children's toys scattered in the front yard. He knocked on the door, and a scantily-dressed woman with a small child behind her opened it.

"What do you want?" she asked with a hint of fear in her voice.

"Please don't be alarmed. I'm Dennis Coleman with the sheriff's department in North Carolina; here's my badge. We're investigating some mysterious circumstances surrounding a man by the name of Degar Loghin. We understand that Eliza Harper lives here, and we need to contact her. Her address was furnished to us by a friend of hers in North Carolina."

"She's my older sister and she went to North Carolina at the request of Degar Loghin. She returned a few weeks ago pretty frightened. I'm worried about her."

"I'd certainly like to see her. Is she here?"

"No, she left about an hour ago to try to get a job in the restaurant where she used to work before she left."

"We'll try to find her. Please don't worry about it; your sister isn't in trouble, but she may be able to give us some information."

With the help of a policeman guide, they found the A & B restaurant, which was a few blocks away from the York Hotel. It was almost lunchtime, so they went in and got a table. A rather pretty waitress arrived promptly.

"I'm Dennis Coleman from the sheriff's department in New Hanover County, North Carolina, and we're looking for a girl named Eliza Harper. She worked here last May and recently moved back to Cincinnati. We understand that she's looking to get her old job back," Dennis said after he had placed his order.

"What do you want with her?"

"Be assured that she's not in any trouble, but her friend's daughter died, and there was some conflict about the cause of death. We want to see if she can give us any helpful information."

"She was here about thirty minutes ago asking to speak to the manager. He wasn't here, and she left. She said she'd come back around noon."

"When she returns, will you ask her to call Dennis Coleman in room 324 at the York Hotel? We'd like to speak to her."

"Sure, I'll be glad to do it, but from what she told me she doesn't want to have anything to do with North Carolina."

After finishing their lunch Eliza and Dennis walked back to the hotel. At about two o'clock the phone rang. Emma answered it.

"This is Eliza Harper, and one of my waitress friends said you'd like to speak to me concerning my visit to Wilmington."

"Yes, Miss Harper, and be assured there's nothing wrong that would cause you any trouble. My husband and I would like to speak to you. Degar Loghin's neighbor gave us your address and told us that you had left it with her in case anyone needed to get in touch with you," Emma said.

"That's right, I did, but I don't know whether I should talk to you or not."

"Why don't we meet you somewhere and see what we can do? I promise you that you're not in trouble."

"That will be fine. Where should we meet?"

"How about meeting us in the lobby of the York Hotel? We can have a cup of coffee and talk. My husband is Dennis Coleman, and I believe you'll find that he's a gentleman."

At 4:30 on the dot, a slim brunette woman dressed in a waitress uniform came through the revolving doors. Emma knew it was Eliza. " I'm Emma Coleman and we spoke together on the telephone. This is my husband, Dennis, with the sheriff's department in Wilmington. The department sent Dennis here to see if you have information that might help in the investigation of Tess Loghin's death. I came along to see if I could help," Emma said.

"I was there when she died, but I don't know what was wrong

with her. She was a sweet kid, but her daddy was hard on her from the day I came to his house."

"How about telling us about it?"

"I'm very ashamed of my behavior. Last May I met Degar at the restaurant, and he snowed me with what I thought was love. We had a little dance around for the few days he was here. About a month later he called and told me that his wife had died. He said if I came down there and helped him with his daughter he'd put me up and provide for me. So I went, and he got me a job at the Orton Hotel on Front Street. He took care of some of my bills and came to see me all the time. It was a better deal than I had here. He came by one Saturday afternoon and said that if I moved into his house and took care of it he'd marry me. He told me that he had a good job at the railroad and could provide for me, and that I could help him look after his young daughter. I agreed and moved in with him.

"His daughter got sick on Thanksgiving Day, and I went to the hospital with them. They pumped out her stomach and released her the next day. A few days later the same symptoms returned and I told the neighbor about it. She called Tess' grandmother, and Mary Mann came the day Tess died. We were both with her at the time, but the doctor we called didn't show up until after she had died. They took her to the hospital, but it was too late."

"Did you see Degar give her anything?"

"Yes. He gave her pills from a bicarbonate of soda jar that he said he'd gotten at the railroad dispensary."

"Do you know what happened to the bottle?"

"No. The doctor asked for it so he could send it off to be

analyzed, and Degar said he would get it . . . but I never saw him give it to him, and I never saw it again.

"He buried Tess shortly thereafter in South Carolina, where he said that her mother was buried. I didn't go with them because I had to work.

"That's all I know about it—except that he seemed to have some extra money shortly after she died. I think it came from life insurance on her, but evidently it wasn't very much. He wouldn't tell me how much. One day while he was at work I looked through a drawer in the living room and found a bunch of insurance policies, including one that had my name on it, with Degar as beneficiary. That's when I got worried and decided to leave. I left without telling him. I thought something might come up, and that's why I gave the neighbor the address here."

"Thank you for all of this information. You've been very helpful, but I have one more question. Did you ever go to a drugstore with him and see him buy anything?" Dennis asked.

"No. He usually left me at home when he went out. Look, I've just been rehired at the restaurant and have to report before six o'clock. I'm running late. Can you give me some money for a cab?"

"Sure, here's two dollars. We have your address and will contact you if you can be of further help."

Dennis and Emma spent a quiet day on Sunday, and went to a local Baptist church. The sermon was based on Luke 17: "Where the corpse lies, the eagles will gather." Dennis thought the verse was appropriate for their visit, as the eagles were certainly gathering and closing in on Degar Loghin.

They took the train back on Monday morning, and strange to say, the curtains on the berth were unbuttoned. Dennis slipped in.

"I love you, Emma."

"I love you, Dennis."

The rhythm of the tracking wheels complemented the symphony of their love.

Chapter Nineteen

As the train backed into the station the two tired travelers reached the concourse to find Sheriff Dawkins waiting for them at the entrance.

"Dennis, you seem to have done a good job, but we have to meet with Bill Odom first thing this morning to start the ball rolling for an indictment."

"That's fine with me, but we'll have to drop Emma at the house first. I'm glad she went with me. I don't believe Eliza Harper would have given me any information. She was very suspect of my badge."

"Emma, we sure do thank you for your help. I'll try to arrange for you and Dennis to have some time together when it doesn't involve investigations." They drove in town, dropped Emma off, and proceeded to Odom's office. He was in his usual position—feet on desk and spittoon nearby.

"Glad to see you back, son. Give me the details so my girl can prepare an affidavit to give to the judge requesting a search warrant—and possibly an order for Tess and Ginny Loghin to be disinterred. I haven't decided yet when we'll go to the grand jury with this, but we'll probably wait."

Dennis outlined the location where the purchase of the strychnine had been made, and the evidence they had obtained from Eliza Harper. This was incorporated into an affidavit along with the evidence regarding the residue found in the dog, Tess and Ginny's strange deaths, the death certificates, and the interviews with the doctors.

They found the resident Superior Court judge holding court in an adjacent county and appeared before him. He was convinced by Odom's presentation, and an order was entered calling for the removal of Ginny's and Tess' bodies from their graves and for an autopsy of each body.

That ended a long morning's work, and they went to lunch together at a small café. They returned and went to the mortuary where they were disappointed to find that Tess Loghin's body had been transported to South Carolina for burial, although Ginny, her stepmother, was buried in the local cemetery. Now they would have to contact the county health department doctor, Dr. John Best, and have him travel with them to do the autopsy, and have the undertaker identify the remains. They called the state's attorney in South Carolina and arranged to appear before a magistrate to obtain a complementary order from the South Carolina court for Tess' body to be disinterred.

It wasn't until the next day that Dawkins, Dennis, Odom, Dr. Best, and the undertaker left for South Carolina. It took four hours to drive to the small town where the burial had taken place. They went to the magistrate's office and he was ready to sign another order at the prompting of the local state's attorney.

It was almost dark when they finally reached the fairly fresh grave, and they used Coleman lanterns to provide light for the gravediggers. Their shovels finally clicked on metal, and the rather small, white casket was uncovered and manhandled to the surface. They removed the lid and their lanterns revealed the body of a young girl.

"This is the body of Tess Loghin. I picked her up at the hospital and placed her in this casket," the Wilmington undertaker said.

"Is it in essentially the same condition as when you last saw it?"

"Yes, the hands and feet are clenched as they were at the time of death. There has been no change."

"Doctor, you'll have to take the body to the local hospital and do an autopsy. Please remove the appropriate organs so that we can send them to Duke University Hospital to determine the amount—if any—of the poisonous residue that may remain," Odom said to Dr. Best.

"I'll have to do it tomorrow. I checked with the hospital this afternoon, and the morgue isn't available to me tonight. The local pathologist will be there to help me tomorrow morning," Best replied. They left Dr. Best and the undertaker with the body at a local funeral home, and Dennis, Odom, and Dawkins drove back home.

The autopsy was performed the next day, and Dr. Best, accompanied by another doctor from town, took parts of the viscera, liver, kidneys, and brain on the train to Durham, North Carolina. They stayed while the pathology department made their tests. The next day a report was returned to Bill Odom, and to no one's surprise, there was evidence of strychnine in Tess' organs.

As soon as Odom received the news he went to the Clerk of Court's office and prepared a warrant for Degar Loghin's arrest on suspicion of first-degree murder of his daughter and wife.

At five o'clock that afternoon Dennis and the Sheriff went to the roundhouse, and as Degar left the premises, served him the warrant. He was arrested, handcuffed, and taken to jail, where he was booked without bond and placed in a cell for later questioning.

The jail was on the top floor of a white marble courthouse building, which had been built behind the old traditional Victorian courthouse. The cells were located up a set of steep stairs, or they could be reached using the elevator that was large enough to carry twelve people. The elevator had safety restraints built in to prevent an attempted escape during transfer. Below the jail was the large Superior Court room that replaced the old courtroom next door. It was close by so that justice or mercy could be conveniently dispensed.

Sheriff Dawkins and Dennis went over early in the morning and were greeted by the jailer, Marion Gloss.

"Good morning. You certainly left me a solemn customer last night. He paced and complained all night and didn't eat any supper. He hardly touched his breakfast, even though I gave him some country ham and grits," Gloss said.

"Well, we need to question him, and after we do, he'll probably have even less of an appetite. Bring him out so we can talk to him. Keep him handcuffed." The somber-looking prisoner was led to a table where he sat down opposite Dennis and Dawkins.

"I don't know why you've got me in here. I want to get out on bond so I can go to my job," Degar said.

"You're here on suspicion of the murder of your wife Ginny, and your daughter Tess," Dawkins said.

135

"What do you mean? They both died of natural causes. I didn't do a thing to them."

"We have reason to believe that they died of strychnine poisoning, even though the doctors didn't recognize it at the time."

"Well don't blame me. I'm just a hardworking mechanic at the railroad who's had the misfortune of losing his daughter and his wife in the last year."

"Did you go to Cincinnati last May for the railroad?"

"Yes, but what's that got to do with it?"

"We have some evidence that you purchased a large amount of strychnine there."

"My dog had worms and I bought it to treat her."

"Yeah, and she died too, shortly thereafter."

"Yeah, the heartworms finally got to her and she did die."

"But that doesn't explain why your wife and daughter died shortly thereafter. The doctors tell us now that it could have been from poison."

"I don't know what the doctors say. They were slow in signing the death certificates, but I didn't have anything to do with what was the matter with them."

"We are told that your first wife died under similar circumstances back in 1922."

"I had nothing to do with her death; she got sick and died."

"Yes, and you collected insurance on all of them."

"I guess you're entitled to collect insurance if you pay the premiums—which I did. People die of natural causes."

"Well, we're going to the grand jury to get a true bill indicting you for the murders, so if you know anything you'd better come clean."

Degar's stoic expression didn't change. "I loved my wife and daughter, took good care of them, and I didn't kill them. Please have a bond set so that I can try to get out of here." That ended the interview, and Dennis and Dawkins noted that Degar had admitted to purchasing strychnine.

The deputies came back from searching Loghin's house and reported that no medicines had been found; the only thing there was a box of bicarbonate of soda and a bunch of clothes, both men's and women's. Most of the furniture was old and in disrepair, and although it had been searched inside and out, nothing of a suspicious nature was uncovered. The locker at the roundhouse and the automobile that had been impounded had likewise revealed no incriminating evidence. They sent the box of soda to be tested.

After they left the jail Dawkins arranged for the exhumation and autopsy of Ginny Loghin's body. He met with District Attorney Odom to tell him about the interview with the prisoner, and to prepare for the grand jury hearing.

Chapter Twenty

The grand jury met on the second floor of the courthouse in a fairly small room. The current jury had been sworn in for one-year terms. The hearings were supposed to be secret, but the vicissitudes of human nature and the natural curiosity of the people around the courthouse continuously threatened this scenario.

Caleb took Jake to the courthouse early that morning after Bill Odom called. When they arrived they took seats outside the jury room. Jake was scared, but Caleb had assured him that he was going to be all right. Dennis and the Sheriff were there, as well as Dr. Best, who had returned from his recent trip to Durham with a bundle of papers with him.

While they were seated in the hall, a tall man dressed in a business suit came by.

"That's the new foreman of the jury. He's an officer at Compress Warehouse, and he'll preside over the proceedings. The district attorney, Bill Odom, will present the evidence we have right now and try to get an indictment," Sheriff Dawkins said. He turned to Jake. "Jake, this is just sort of a preliminary hearing of the evidence that is available at this time about the death of your friend Tess. Later there'll be a full court hearing with a judge to rule on the evidence, and a jury to determine whether Degar Loghin is guilty."

"Will I have to go to the big court?"

"That will be decided later. There's a lot to do before we get to that point."

"I sure hope they find out what killed Tess."

Bill Odom arrived and said good morning and, as he entered the courtroom, a number of people—men and women—followed him.

About ten minutes later he reappeared. "Jake, I guess we'll start off with you. Come on in and I'll ask you a few questions."

Jake was amazed at the courtroom's somber appearance. The foreman introduced himself. "Jake, I'm John Christian, and I work at the Compress Warehouse. I'm serving as a citizen, as we all are, and as foreman of this group. The district attorney will ask you a few questions after you're sworn in. We're here to decide whether there's enough evidence for Degar Loghin to be indicted and placed on trial for the death of Tess Loghin." Jake took a seat in a chair near the foreman.

"You're Jake Jones, and you were a friend of Tess Loghin, is that right?" Odom began.

"Yes, we were in every school class from the first grade on, and from time to time we were together in school activities. She was a good friend and lived down the road from me."

"Did you ever date her?"

"Yes, we went to some school activities and dances together."

"Tell us about how she behaved."

"Tess was always timid, and she told me that she was afraid of her daddy. She said he always threatened her when she came from school or from a school function."

"Did she tell you about the death of their dog?"

"Yes, one day at school, Tess said that her dog, Sis, had died the night before, and she asked me to help her bury it. We found the dog in the back yard, put it in a croaker sack, then took it across the road and dug a hole. We buried it there. Later Dennis Coleman and some men got me and they dug it up. It smelled bad, and there were worms all over the sack that we had buried it in."

The foreman asked a few more questions, told Jake that he shouldn't talk to anyone about his testimony, and thanked him.

Odom presented testimony regarding the strychnine found in the dog. Dennis and Sheriff Dawkins testified about the findings in Cincinnati, including Loghin's purchase there and the interview with Eliza Harper. Dawkins also told the jury about the dog, Tess' exhumation, and the toxicologist's report. A doctor testified that he believed Tess' death could have been caused by strychnine poisoning. He also said that they had exhumed Ginny Loghin's body and were waiting for a toxicology report on her remains. Odom said that if Ginny's body showed evidence of strychnine he would seek another indictment for her death in July.

Odom then addressed the jury in his most gentle and accommodating manner, asking them to return a true bill charging Degar Loghin with murder in the first degree. That afternoon the following was sent to his office:

The jurors for the State, upon their oath, do present that Degar Loghin, late of this County, on the first day of December 1936, with force and arms, at and in this County, feloniously, willfully, and with malice aforethought, did kill and murder Tess Loghin, contrary to the form of the statute, in such case made and provided, against the peace and dignity of the State.

An indictment was issued in the same language.

Odom rubbed his hands together with glee. He knew that he could win this case and that it would become a turning point in his career.

The next morning the indictment hit the newspaper, and it was the main subject of discussion at the railroad, particularly in the "zoo," where Jere Swain was devastated by the news. The paper reported that Degar was held without bond and did not have an attorney or money to hire one, and Jere wondered if he should try to raise some money to help him. He went to the roundhouse after work and found Bob Callus, the foreman, and they discussed the matter.

"We'll surely miss Degar if he doesn't get back to work. I don't have anyone else I can count on," said Callus.

"Do you think that you could raise some money to help him hire a lawyer?"

"He was always a quiet person and a loner. I don't know that he had many friends here, but I'll talk around and see if we can raise a bit."

A few days later, Degar was arraigned before the local Superior Court judge and entered a plea of "not guilty" through his court-appointed attorney, Bill Gardener. He was again remanded to jail without bond.

In the meantime Callus had raised $175 for Degar's defense fund, which, with the $150 Jere had raised, made a total of $325. Jere took the money to Joshua Clayton, a veteran criminal lawyer with an office near the courthouse. He had to wait a while, but upon entering Clayton's office, he found the grizzled lawyer smoking a cigar.

"I'm Jere Swain, a friend of Degar Loghin, and I would like to hire you to defend him."

"Well, from what I read in the papers, the whole case has been leaked from the courthouse and he may have already been convicted in the public eye," Clayton replied.

"We've raised some money to pay a lawyer and would like to hire you."

"Well, I see he already has a young man named Gardener to defend him. I couldn't come in without his permission. I require a $500 retainer to get into the case."

"We have only raised $325, but could probably get a little more to help out."

"All right, just leave the money here and I'll call Gardener to see if he agrees. I'll try to assist him if you can raise fifty dollars more."

Jere said he would try and gave Clayton his telephone number. Back at the railroad Legal department he spoke to Bill David and requested his help. When he entered David's office he got straight to the point and related the entire situation. "You may remember that Degar's the one who testified favorably for us in the case where the switchman was killed in the roundhouse."

"Yes I remember. It saved us a lot of money."

"I think it would be a good idea to help him."

"It's not the policy of the company to help employees in criminal matters, but the foreman called me and said that Loghin was very important to him. I may be able to get the fifty dollars you need."

"Call me tomorrow."

At home that night Jere received a call from Clayton saying that Gardener had agreed to work with him on Degar's defense and that they thought the court would approve it. The next day Jere delivered the additional fifty dollars to Clayton. It would be impossible to obtain Degar's release on bond. No bond had been set, and it was very rare for the court to set bond in a first-degree murder case.

Jere was pleased with what he had done for his friend, but was very disturbed by the news that was being published in the paper every day. The latest included a statement that the prosecutors were seeking an additional indictment for the death of Degar's wife.

Chapter Twenty-one

I t was a gloomy, rainy day as Clayton and Gardener walked toward the courthouse for their first joint interview with their client. They climbed the front steps of the building and entered the elevator. A sheriff's deputy exited with a handcuffed prisoner as they entered, and they ascended to the third floor where the jail was located. When they stepped out of the elevator they were greeted by the stale smell of cooking grease mixed with the odor of sweat. At their request the jailer on duty showed them into the room where Loghin, still handcuffed, sat at a small table.

Gardener opened. "Degar, this is Joshua Clayton. Some of your friends have hired him to help me defend you. We'll be working together, and I hope we can do you a good service."

"I need a lot of help, but first I need to know if you can get me out on bond."

"No, that's impossible," replied Clayton. "The court won't set bond in a first-degree murder case, and, as you know, if you're convicted the death penalty will be imposed."

Loghin's dark countenance whitened a bit. "I didn't kill anybody. I'm innocent," he said stoically.

"Sometimes it's better to come out with the truth," said Clayton. "If you tell us exactly what happened we might be able to reach an agreement with the D.A. It could save you from an embarrassing trial and the possibility of ending your life in the death chamber."

"Yeah, but I still might be in jail for a long time, and I need to get back to work at the roundhouse."

"What do you think caused Tess' death?"

"Well, she didn't take care of herself and had too much to eat at Thanksgiving. Then she had the same thing happen later, and I guess it was too much for her."

"Did you give her anything?"

"Only bicarbonate of soda and B.C. Powders, both of which I got from the railroad dispensary when she complained of indigestion."

"The State claims you gave her strychnine that you purchased on a trip you made to Ohio."

"That was to worm my dog Sis, and for some hogs I was planning to purchase and raise in my yard. The dog died shortly after that because of the worms."

"Why do you think your wife died?"

"Well, she was going to have a baby and had a lot of morning sickness. I guess it finally caught up with her and she was just too weak to recover. I miss my little girl and Ginny."

"What would you say if the evidence shows that there was strychnine in their bodies after they died?"

"I certainly didn't give it to them. I don't know how it could have happened. I kept the strychnine in my locker at the railroad. I don't know how they could have got it, but I certainly didn't give it to them and didn't kill them!"

The two advocates left with many questions still unanswered. They agreed that if Degar continued with his absolute denials they would have to go to trial and hope that something would turn up to vindicate him.

In the meantime Odom had gone to the grand jury and obtained an indictment for Ginny Loghin's death, again for first-degree murder. After a discussion with Sheriff Dawkins and Dennis he decided not to consolidate the two cases. He'd wait to see how they came out with Tess before proceeding with the other case.

"You know," said Odom, "we're probably not ever going to get direct evidence that he administered the strychnine to Tess. We'll have to have enough circumstantial evidence to convince the jury beyond a reasonable doubt that he did it. This may be hard; juries are best convinced by hard facts, which we may not have."

"We have yet to agree on a motive that we can prove," Dennis added.

"The existence of insurance is important, but the policies were so small . . . . It may be hard to prove that someone would commit murder for such a small amount of money," Odom said.

"You noticed that the toxicology report on Ginny Loghin indicated that she was three to four months pregnant. We know Loghin saw Eliza Harper in Cincinnati and had a little dance around with her. Maybe he didn't want more children."

"That's a pretty gruesome way to take care of birth control," said Sheriff Dawkins.

"Of course, he wanted to bring Eliza down and that would have been hard to do with Ginny still around the house," said Odom. "Although we have three possibilities, I believe insurance is the main motive. You have to realize that even though the amounts are small, times are mighty hard. Extra money can make a lot of difference right now. One major problem we have in setting the court case for trial is getting the druggist and Eliza Harper down here to testify. I'll need to get them here in time to make sure they'll be ready to testify. I also need to decide whether the druggist will identify Loghin as the purchaser of the strychnine."

More conversation followed. They discussed having the local authorities in Ohio serve subpoenas on Eliza and the druggist and having them accompany the witnesses to Wilmington for the trial. This would require extra expense, but it would certainly be approved considering the seriousness of the case and the already-overenthusiastic media.

Dennis left the conference very perplexed, but he was confident that Bill Odom would prove his case. When he got home Emma welcomed him with a big kiss. She informed him that she had a new dress and that they were going to the beach for a special winter dance at the big pavilion. The weather had been warm that January and the dance was scheduled to take advantage of it.

Dennis shed his uniform, put on his best coat and tie, and was ready to go very quickly. Emma was slow to dress, trying to enhance her appearance to please him as much as possible.

They walked to the beach car line and paid fifty cents to get aboard. In the near darkness they were transported to the large wooden pavilion at the south end of the beach. Upon entering, they could hear the soft tunes of Al Katz and his Kittens wafting from the top floor. With Emma in his arms Dennis was completely content that happiness would be with them forever.

At the intermission, a friend had a ninety-five-cent pint of blended "Carstairs for the Man Who Cares," and gave Dennis a small portion laced with Coke, which added to the exuberance of the evening.

After two hours they wearily returned to the trolley for the trip home, stopping briefly at a soda shop near the beach. On the ride home, Emma spoke quietly to Dennis. "I went to the doctor today. We're to become a family of three sometime in the fall. I shouldn't have left the berth curtains unbuttoned on our return trip from Cincinnati, but I'm glad I did. I love you."

Dennis was happy, too, but the emotional moment left him without words. In the midst of tragedy, new life arises.

Chapter Twenty-two

The sheriff of Hamilton County, Ohio, Bob Yokum, arrived at his office early on Monday morning. He had spent the weekend investigating what he thought was a drowning. It turned out that the child had gone off with some friends and was fine. Confronting two distressed parents had been trying, but finding the child made it worthwhile.

Yokum looked at the special-delivery letter on his desk and opened it. It was a letter from Odom, along with two subpoenas from the Superior Court. His immediate thought was that these people would never accept the subpoenas and voluntarily go to North Carolina. He knew Will Jackson, the pharmacist at Doctor's Drugstore, and the name Eliza Harper seemed vaguely familiar to him. The letter noted that New Hanover County would bear all the expense of getting Harper and Jackson to Wilmington and back home. Eliza was wanted as a material witness; they offered to apply for immunity should she desire it. There was also a check for $1,000 to be applied toward expenses incurred. There was a sense of urgency in the letter. The trial was to be set for the last week in February and it was already late January.

Yokum called his first deputy and asked him to go talk to Eliza and Will Jackson. "Please be careful with these potential witnesses. We don't want them to be uncooperative. You'll probably have to handle them with kid gloves," he said.

When the deputy reached the drugstore and explained the situation to Will Jackson, the pharmacist was very cooperative. "I was expecting to hear some more about this from the calls I've had. I'm prepared to go if and when the arrangements are made and if my expenses are paid," he said.

In the meantime Yokum had someone look to see if there was any record of Emma Harper in the office. She'd had a few spats with the law concerning her frequenting the red light district about three years back, but had served no time. He made a note of this so that he could relay the information to Odom. Since he thought that Eliza Harper might be somewhat suspicious, Yokum decided to contact her himself. He called the number at the address given him and a female voice answered. "She's not here, but she's working at the A & B restaurant. She goes on duty at about four o'clock in the afternoon."

"Thank you. I'll try to contact her there." He found her at the restaurant later that afternoon.

"You must be looking for me about the mistake I made in going to North Carolina with that railroad man," she told Yokum. "He sweet-talked me into going there to marry him. He seemed so nice at the time, and I needed to find some security in these hard times. But the way he treated his daughter . . . her sudden illness . . . scared me. When I heard there was a deputy looking around his house and an investigation, I decided I had better come back home."

Yokum explained the purpose of his visit. Eliza looked at him for a moment and then shifted her eyes to the ground.

"Well, you know I was in trouble with your office some years ago, but it didn't amount to anything. I'd like to have my lawyer look into this. If I'm to have immunity I'll be glad to go and tell what I know—which isn't much—but without immunity I won't go."

Yokum called Odom and asked him to cable a statement that Eliza would have immunity. The next morning Yokum met Eliza in her lawyer's office and the final agreement was made.

Several days later Sheriff Dawkins and Dennis were meeting again in Odom's office.

"We're certainly going to have to get the druggist down here, along with Eliza Harper to get this case to trial. I sent a special delivery letter to the sheriff in Cincinnati with subpoenas. He's served the subpoenas, but it won't matter unless they agree to come down voluntarily. He's going to call me when the arrangements have been completed, provided I get Eliza Harper a grant of immunity, which I will.

"I'm going to request a special court session for the last week of February to try this case. It'll take some time, and if it's set at a regular term the docket may be full. Looking over my notes, I see that Dennis talked to a druggist named Darden on Ninth Street and that he said someone tried to purchase strychnine from him within the last year. Dennis, I want you to take this lineup picture out to Darden and see if he recognizes Degar. If he does, it may help. I also want you to arrange to take him up to the jailhouse and have a look at Degar. It could mean local evidence, which will help."

"I'll do it this afternoon and arrange to take him by the cell block to have a look at Loghin in person."

Dennis took the photograph and drove to the small drugstore on the corner of Ninth and Dock streets. The druggist was named Ned Darden, and he was interested in the story that Dennis told him. He looked at the photograph. "I'm not sure since he had a hat on at the time, but I'll be glad to have a look," Darden said.

"Why don't we meet in my office at about four o'clock and I'll arrange for us to go to the jail?"

"That's fine with me. I get off at about that time," Darden responded.

The meeting took place, and they went to the top-floor jail and walked back and forth in front of the cells.

"It certainly could have been the man, but he was wearing a hat at the time and the light wasn't too good. It looked like him, but I can't be sure. Maybe in better light I can tell," said Darden.

"Thank you, Mr. Darden. I'll tell the district attorney, and if we need you, I'll let you know." Later that day Dennis went to Odom's office and reported what had happened.

A few days later the sheriff in Cincinnati called to say that he had delivered the subpoenas and that both of the witnesses would be available. He reiterated that New Hanover County would have to bear all of the expense for travel, as well as room and board. He indicated that the druggist, Will Jackson, was looking forward to a trip to the South, but that Emma Harper was a little uncertain

Chapter Twenty-three

Joshua Clayton and Bill Gardener were meeting in Clayton's office on another gloomy February afternoon.

"I've had another call from Loghin, and he wants to talk to us again. I don't know why. We saw him day before yesterday and he still maintained his innocence, but there seems to be no chance of avoiding a trial," said Clayton.

"Yes, and Bill Odom has almost received permission for a special session at the end of this month for the sole purpose of trying this case."

"He has no previous criminal record. Our only chance, other than his denial, is to introduce evidence of his good character."

"But that can't help us with the evidence of poison found in the bodies. I'm sure Odom has the bit in his teeth about the insurance policies he collected after their deaths. We can argue that the small amounts wouldn't provide sufficient motive, but times are hard, and one hundred dollars here and there makes a lot of difference these days."

"We've got a tough case, and a client who is almost stoic in about coming. She was still scared of Degar and didn't want to be named as an accomplice.

Odom assured him. "She'll be treated as a material witness. I'll prepare a grant of immunity and provide security for her while she's here. This office will also take care of all expenses, including the expense of her lawyer if he decides to come with her."

It would cost about $1,500 to cover the train tickets, lodging, and food while the witnesses were present for the trial. Odom applied to the court administration for the special term, and the trial was scheduled to commence on the last Monday in February. Since it was already the last week in January, Odom had a full job to get ready.

his denials," added Gardener. "Let's go up and see him again today and try to find something that may help."

They left and walked over to the courthouse, both somewhat chagrined at the task that had been put before them, but realizing, as lawyers, that they must use their best efforts to help their incarcerated client. The elevator ascended slowly, and as it neared the top the smell of the jail and the usual damp, acrid food aroma wafted into the enclosure. They entered and the deputy on duty brought the prisoner to the small conference table.

Clayton opened the interview. "Well, Degar, the district attorney has requested a special session of court to try your case, and he has a large number of witnesses to testify against you. So far he has the druggist who allegedly sold you the strychnine, the insurance agents, the toxicologist who found the poison in the bodies, the doctors who treated Tess and Ginny, and others who will give opinions on the effect of the poison. We only have you, and your denial is certainly a good defense—that is, if you can stand up under the severe cross-examination you'll receive if you testify. You're not required to testify, and if you don't it can't be argued that your refusal is an indication of your guilt. But we must tell you that even though the jury will be instructed to the contrary, human nature is such that your failure to testify will place doubt of your innocence in their minds. If you don't testify, and we offer no other evidence, we'll receive the right to make the closing argument to the jury, which has some advantage, but that will put the complete responsibility for your life in our hands, and you have to realize that."

"I want to testify and let the jury hear that I'm innocent."

"Yes, but Degar, you've not provided us with the names of

any witnesses who can attest to your innocence, or provide us with evidence which would tend to vindicate you. So it will boil down to your denial tested against the circumstantial and coincidental evidence, which seems to us to be pretty strong. We must advise you of this, and unless some plea arrangement is made, you'll surely face the death penalty. Bill Odom has plenty of ambition to put you away in order to enhance his future in the legal profession."

Degar was silent for a moment. "You've explained the seriousness of this to me before, but I didn't kill Tess or Ginny, and you tell me that the search warrants didn't reveal any poison in the house or around the premises. The dog I admit, but if they were poisoned, I have no idea of how they received it."

"There is one good thing we have. You have no previous criminal record. We can also put on evidence of the character and reputation that you have in the community. Do you have any witnesses we can get to testify to this?" Clayton asked.

"Yes, my friend Jere Swain, Bob Callus the foreman at the shop, and also a neighbor or two who I believe will testify."

Gardener made a note to issue subpoenas for these and others. "We believe that Odom will attempt to bring Eliza Harper down here to testify. We know his man has been up there to interview her. Could she possibly know anything?"

"No, I don't think so. I brought her down to keep house for me after Ginny died, and she hadn't been there long. I don't know what she could say. I hoped to marry her, but she just up and left shortly after Tess died."

"Well, we'll be working on the case all month, so have the jailer call us anytime that you have ideas and we'll come over. In the meantime, I hope they're taking good care of you here," said Gardener.

"Please keep trying to get me out on bond. I need to look after my house, and try to earn a little money."

They left the jail and went back to the office as confused as before. The case seemed hopeless and the death penalty wasn't far away.

"You know Odom's obtained an indictment in the death of Ginny Loghin," said Gardener, "and the court clerk told me that he won't try the two cases together. We can object to any evidence that he tries to inject about Ginny's death."

They discussed this further and decided that they would go and see Jere Swain. They had received some information at the railroad that Jere had been on the trip to Cincinnati shortly before Degar's wife died.

The local newspaper had, of course, dogged the district attorney and the defense counsel with many questions about the case. As a result the front page had been full of stories and implications. The nickname "Poison Master" was used frequently to refer to Degar. Gardener and Clayton wondered whether he could get a fair trial in the county, and considered moving for a change of venue, or at least requesting that the jurors be obtained from an adjoining county.

They found Jere Swain at his home, and Clayton advised the purpose of their visit. Swain was reluctant to talk at first, but when he understood that they were trying to get information to help Degar, he opened up.

"He's a very good friend of mine, and I was shocked to hear about the case. We went to the train wreck together and stayed in

Cincinnati at the same hotel. We had separate rooms and I only saw him in the mornings. I was trying to handle the cotton, and he was going to try to get the boxcars back in running order. We had dinner together at a restaurant one night, and he was friendly with one of the waitresses, but I don't know what happened after that, as I went home early. I didn't see him go to a drugstore, nor did he tell me of any purchases he'd made except aspirin."

"When you went fishing, did he speak of his wife or daughter?"

"He was still sad over his wife's death, and said that Tess was helping at the house, and that he hoped to get a housekeeper soon."

"Could you testify to his good character?"

"I'll be glad to."

They left and visited Bob Callus, the foreman at the shop, and he agreed to try to help.

When they returned to the office, they prepared a motion for a change of venue and sent it to the courthouse for filing. The basis for the motion was that the trial could not be fair because of the publicity.

The local press had published much information about the investigation and the pending trial, and the wire services had picked it up. The case was receiving national publicity. Loghin had been described as a "serial poison killer," who had put away his wife and child with systematic and cruel skill. Ginny and Tess' deaths were described as agonizing, and since poison was allegedly used, the reports went as far as to accuse Degar of premeditation and planning.

Chapter Twenty-four

After reading the motion for a change of venue, and the affidavits that accompanied it, the court ruled that the trial should be in the county of Degar's residence, and since he worked at the railroad, he should be able to receive a fair trial. In a bit of a compromise, the judge directed that some of the jury panel be obtained from the adjoining county to assure that they hadn't been affected by the media coverage.

On the morning that the trial opened with Judge William Clawson presiding, the courtroom was packed with onlookers who had come early to obtain a seat. The court had to limit those admitted to the seats available, allowing no standing spectators.

The selection of the jury took most of the first day, and many of those on the panel asked to be excused because they expressed opposition to the death penalty. Also, a number of railroad employees were reluctant to serve in judgment of their fellow worker. In any event, after much questioning and positioning by the prosecution and the defendant's attorneys, a jury of twelve plus two alternates was sworn in. The judge also directed Sheriff

Dawkins to obtain hotel accommodations so that the jury could be sequestered during the trial and not be exposed to the expected publicity. Because of the visibility the case had garnered, there were also reporters from other parts of the state—and even out of state—in attendance. Because no press facilities were available they were seated throughout the audience.

Degar Loghin, seated at the defendant's table between his two attorneys, was dressed in a suit and tie, which highlighted his stoic appearance. From time to time during the jury selection, he would confer with Joshua Clayton, and apparently give him some suggestions with regard to the juror being interviewed. Beyond that he sat quietly, rigidly paying attention to the proceedings, but showing little emotion.

There was some time left in the first afternoon, so the judge ordered the prosecution to begin. There were no opening statements or arguments. The judge was of the opinion that the jurors had absorbed enough information about the case from the interrogations.

The bailiff read the indictment and Odom introduced his first witness, Mary Mann.

"Would you please state your name and address?"

"I'm Mary Mann, my husband was Bailey Mann. I'm Tess' grandmother and live in South Carolina."

"How long have you known the defendant, Degar Loghin?"

"He married my daughter in 1918, and I knew him shortly before that time while they were dating."

"When was Tess Loghin born?"

"She was born in 1921, and my daughter died shortly thereafter. Tess came down and lived with Bailey and me until Degar took her back up here after he had married the second time."

"Were you present when your daughter died?"

"Yes. She was very sick, and Degar was there with her. She was suffering and told Degar that she thought she'd been poisoned. Degar said that he thought she might have been, too."

Joshua Clayton objected and was overruled.

"What happened then?"

"She died shortly after that and was buried, and as I stated, Tess stayed with us a while after that."

"When did Tess leave?"

"A few months later Degar remarried and came and got her. He told us that he and his new wife could take care of her."

"Did you see Tess after that from time to time?"

"Yes, whenever I came up here I would always try to see her."

"Do you know the condition of her health?"

"Yes, it was generally good except for the usual childhood diseases. She was always a little thin."

"On or about December first of last year did you have occasion to see Tess?"

"Yes, I received a phone call and came up here to the house. When I went in, I could hear moaning from the bedroom, and she was there on the bed calling for someone to help her. We called Degar, but he didn't come. We called Dr. Williams to come, but before he got there Tess died. There was nothing he could do."

"Describe her physical condition as you observed it."

"She was lying on the bed, kind of bent over, and her head was pulled back. Her arms and legs were extended and her hands were clenched. When she looked at me she didn't seem to know who I was . . . .it just broke my heart."

"What was Eliza Harper doing?"

"She was trying to comfort her and had a moist towel on her head. She tried to give her water, but Tess couldn't drink it."

"Did you see any medicine there?"

"There was a bottle of something on the table by the bed, but when Degar came I saw him pick it up. I don't know what happened to it."

"Did you help with the funeral arrangements?"

"No. Degar told me that he wanted her buried in South Carolina near his mother, and before I knew anything, the casket had been sent there by train. I didn't attend the funeral."

"What did you do after that?"

"Well, I didn't like what had gone on, so I went to the sheriff's office and told Dennis Coleman about what had happened. I asked him to look into it. He called me from time to time and told me what was going on." Odom had no further questions.

Bill Gardener began his cross-examination. "Mrs. Mann, Tess was your granddaughter?"

"Yes."

"But you lived in South Carolina and only saw her occasionally?"

"Yes."

"So you weren't familiar with whether or not she had been sick, or what she may have had to eat that day?"

"No."

"You've stated that her general health was good, but you weren't familiar with it on a day-to-day basis?"

"That's true, but I never heard that she had health problems."

"So as far as you know her sickness could have been caused

162

by any number of things?"

"Yes."

"No further questions."

When court adjourned that day both Odom and Clayton were accosted by a crowd of about one hundred people with questions about the proceedings. Neither of them made any comment, and while the crowd was shouting at them they crossed the street to their offices.

Degar was hustled to the elevator by the bailiff and taken back to the top-floor jail.

Chapter Twenty-five

The next morning Odom called the undertaker, Bill Woolvin, to the stand. "On December first were you called to the hospital to pick up a body?"

"Yes, it was in the afternoon. I don't remember who called me, but I believe it was the father of the young girl, Degar Loghin."

"What was the condition of the body?"

"She was a girl of about fifteen years of age. She had her hands clenched and her feet extended. From her appearance I estimated she had been dead for about four hours."

"What did you do then?"

"I spoke to her father, who had a small burial policy with an insurance company, and he asked me to take the body to the funeral home and arrange to ship it to South Carolina for burial. I took the body, but the hospital had a problem finding someone who would sign the death certificate. I had to have the certificate before the body could be embalmed or buried."

"How did you get the death certificate?"

"I had to go back to the hospital and find Dr. Champion,

who had treated the girl on Thanksgiving. Dr. Williams, who had seen her shortly after her death, wouldn't sign it. Dr. Champion finally signed it, giving the cause of death as 'idiopathic convulsions'."

Odom passed him a piece of paper. "Is this the death certificate you finally received?"

"Yes."

Odom identified it as an exhibit. "Did you then embalm the body at that point?"

"Yes, using a formaldehyde solution. It was placed in a casket, and I prepared to ship it to South Carolina on December third. For some reason, Loghin seemed anxious to send the body south as soon as possible."

Clayton objected and moved to strike the testimony on the basis that it was speculation, and the judge sustained the objection. The jury was instructed not to consider it.

"What did you do after you talked to Degar Loghin?"

"We shipped the casket with the body to South Carolina the next day."

"After it was shipped south, did you have occasion to see it again?"

"Yes. A week or so later I went to a cemetery in South Carolina with you, the sheriff, and Dr. Best. We were led to a fairly fresh grave and the casket was uncovered. I recognized it as the casket we had furnished. When we opened it the body was in about the same condition it was in when it left my place. I recognized it as the body of Tess Loghin. She was taken to the local hospital where Dr. Best did an autopsy and removed certain organs."

"Are you sure that it was Tess Loghin's body?"

"Absolutely."

"Did you arrange the funeral of Degar Loghin's wife, Ginny Loghin?"

"Yes in July of last year I saw the body of Ginny Loghin. Her body was very tense. Her hands were clenched and her feet were turned downward with the toes inclined inward."

"At a later date did you attend the exhumation of Ginny Loghin's body?"

"Yes. I clearly recognized her, even though there had been some changes due to decomposition."

"What was done with this body?"

"Dr. Best also took it to the hospital here and did an autopsy and removed some organs."

"And you are absolutely sure it was Ginny Loghin's body?"

"Yes."

He handed the witness a paper. "Is this the death certificate of Ginny Loghin?"

"Yes." It was identified as an exhibit and placed in evidence.

"What does it indicate as cause of death?"

"Heart ailment."

"No further questions."

Clayton began the cross-examination. "Isn't it true that when rigor mortis sets in the hands and limbs may become clenched and extended as a result?"

"Yes, I've seen that happen."

"So you don't really know what caused this condition in Tess' body, do you?"

"No."

"Have you ever seen a death certificate before showing 'idiopathic convulsions' as the cause of death?"

"No."

"So doesn't it indicate that the doctor didn't know what caused the death?"

"I guess so." Odom's motion to strike was allowed.

"Do you know what happened to the organs after they were removed?"

"No, Dr. Best took them."

"And so far as you know Ginny Loghin died of heart trouble?"

"Yes, that's true."

"You may step down."

Jake Jones was called to the stand. He was dressed in his corduroy pants and a sweater, and his mother had insisted that he wear a tie. He looked very uneasy, but took the oath and faced Bill Odom.

"Did you know Tess Loghin?"

"Yes, we were in the first grade together, and in school all the way up to high school when she no longer came to school."

"What was your relationship with her?"

"We were good friends. She lived a short way down the road from where I lived. We went to school activities together and I had a few dates with her."

"Did she ever request your help?"

"Yes. She had an old hound called Sis, and when it died she asked me to help her bury it. We took it across the highway and buried it near where I had buried my dog."

"What was the condition of the dog?"

"It was all stiff and its legs were extended. We put it in a burlap bag and buried it."

"Were you present when the dog was exhumed?"

"Yes. I took Mr. Dennis Coleman there. When they dug it up it was covered with worms, but they still took it away."

"Are you sure that it was the same dog?"

"Yes."

There was no cross-examination, but Joshua Clayton moved to strike all of this testimony as being immaterial and irrelevant. His motion was overruled.

A local toxicologist then testified that he examined the organs of the dog, and that there was a residue of strychnine in them.

Odom announced that he had two witnesses coming from Cincinnati and that they would be in on the train the next morning. He requested that the court adjourn until the next day. Clayton and Gardener both objected but were overruled and the adjournment was entered.

The newspaper headline the next morning caused an uproar:

SECRET WITNESSES TO ARRIVE FROM OHIO
IN LOGHIN CASE!

A speculative story followed citing the possible testimony of the witnesses. This typified the spectacular coverage throughout the trial.

Chapter Twenty-six

The train arrived on time the next morning, and Will Jackson, Eliza Harper, and a deputy from Ohio descended to the platform. Dennis and Emma were there to meet them. Dennis took Will to Odom's office, and Emma took Eliza and the deputy to the Orton Hotel. Jackson had the original page from the pharmacy's registry book. Emma told Eliza that she was to meet with Odom at lunchtime and that she wouldn't be called to testify until later in the afternoon. Will Jackson was to take the witness stand in the morning, and his testimony and cross-examination would take some time.

Odom started that day's session by putting Ed Darden on the stand.

"I'm a druggist with a store at Ninth and Dock Steets, and I've been serving the public from there for about fifteen years."

"Do you sell poisonous drugs?"

"Not on a regular basis, but sometimes we order them for regular customers."

"On or about the first of May last year did you have an

inquiry about the purchase of strychnine at your store?"

"Yes at about six o'clock a man came in wearing a hat. He asked if I had strychnine for sale."

"What did you tell him?"

"That I didn't have it."

"Do you recognize that man in the courtroom today?"

"Yes. He's seated at the table over there." Darden pointed at Degar.

"No further questions."

Gardener addressed the witness. "Are you sure he's the man?"

"Fairly sure."

"But not completely sure?"

"That's right, there are a lot of men in and out of the store."

"No further questions."

The court took a short recess and Odom conferred with Will Jackson for about fifteen minutes. Jackson seemed quite nervous on the stand and he spoke with a strong Yankee accent.

"My name is Will Jackson, and I live in Cincinnati, Ohio. I'm a druggist by trade and work in the Doctor's Drugstore near the hotel downtown."

"Does your store stock strychnine?"

"Yes, we have orders for it from time to time."

"On the thirteenth of May last year did you have occasion to sell it?"

"Yes. Fairly late in the evening, when we were about to close, a man came in and wanted to buy fifty milligrams of strychnine."

"What did you tell him?"

"That the law required him to sign the drug register and give the reason for the purchase."

"Did he sign it?"

"Yes, he signed it D. Loughlin and gave his reason as worming his dog and using it to clean his hogs. He gave his address at the York Hotel." Jackson handed Odom a piece of paper that was identified as the original page in the drug registry.

"Have you seen the man since?"

"No, sir."

"Do you see him here today?"

Jackson pointed at Degar. "Yes, he's seated at the table there."

"No further questions."

Clayton started his cross-examination in a soft and gentle manner. "There are a lot of people coming in and out of your store, are there not?"

"Yes."

"And you have had others purchase strychnine from time to time?"

"Yes."

"Well, then, how do you remember this purchase so well?"

"I remember it because at the same time he bought a package of Trojans, and I thought it was an unusual purchase." A rumble of ribald laughter passed through those seated in the courtroom, whereupon the judge banged his gavel on the bench and called for order.

"Another disturbance like this and the room will be vacated except for the participants in the trial," he barked.

Clayton, although visibly upset by the answer, continued. "Was anyone with him at the time?"

"Yes, there was a girl with him, but she stood outside of the store and took no part in the purchase."

The witness was released, and the court adjourned for lunch.

At lunchtime Bill Odom and Dennis went over to the Orton Hotel and met with Eliza Harper and Emma. It was the first time that Odom had met Eliza, and he approached her in a quiet and gentle manner. He went over her testimony with her, particularly emphasizing the necessity for her to tell the truth, and not to be afraid of any intense cross-examination.

When court reopened, she was placed on the stand. She gave her name, stated that she lived in Cincinnati, and Odom began questioning her. "When did you meet Degar Loghin?"

"He came to the restaurant where I worked in Cincinnati and I waited on his table. He seemed very nice, and after I got off work he met me and we went to a bar and had some drinks. He told me that he was lonely because his wife was going to have a baby, and that he might need someone to come and help him since his teenage daughter was in school."

"Did you see him again?"

"Yes, I saw him the next day, which was my day off. We went out together."

"Did you go to a drugstore?"

"Yes, we went to Doctor's Drug Company and Degar made a purchase. I didn't hear the conversation between him and the druggist since I was outside, but when we left he had a package with him. Later he tried to get me to go to his hotel room and have relations with him, but I refused to go. I saw him twice again, and we became pretty good friends. Frankly, I was attracted to him."

"After he left, did you hear from him?"

"Yes. I was very surprised when I received a letter from him

172

sometime in July. He told me that his wife had died suddenly, and that if I would come down there he could get me a job at a restaurant at a hotel and I could help him keep his house. He also said that his daughter was not doing a very good job for him and that I could help."

"What did you tell him?"

"That if he would send me the money for a ticket and arrange for a place to stay, that I would come on a trial basis to see about it."

"Did you go?"

"Yes. He sent me the money, and said he had arranged for me to have a job at the Orton Hotel dining room, and that they had a place for employees to stay. It sounded like a good deal to me, so I came down here sometime in early August."

"What happened then?"

"I liked the job at the Orton, and I saw him pretty regularly. He suggested that he would like to marry me, and I was interested since we got along pretty well. So to make a long story short, I left the Orton and moved into his house on Beach Road in October. His daughter Tess seemed to resent me being there, but since I relieved some of her chores we at least put up with each other."

"Did he still want to marry you?"

"Yes, and we were planning on it."

"Did you have sexual relations while living in his house?"

"Yes."

"Will you tell us what happened on Thanksgiving?"

"Tess and I had prepared a dinner with turkey and all the trimmings. She had been complaining of indigestion for the last three or four days, and he had given her some pills that he said came from the railroad dispensary. We went to ride in the car, and she became violently ill; she was having some sort of convulsion. We took her to a doctor's house, but he couldn't treat her. He called another doctor and sent her to the hospital. They pumped out her stomach and gave her a shot; she improved and was released the next day. When she came home she seemed all right."

"Did you see the pills again?"

"Yes, Degar had them in his pocket at the hospital and the nurse wanted to have them checked out, but he didn't give them to her. He said he would take care of it."

"Did he take them home?"

"Yes, he had them back at the house and they were available, but I don't know whether he gave anymore to Tess or not."

"Tell us what happened on the first of December."

"Well, Tess didn't improve much, and after he had gone to work that morning she was terribly sick. Her grandmother came to the house and told me that a neighbor had called her about Tess. Tess was in great pain, and we called for a doctor, but about that time she quieted down. When Dr. Williams arrived he checked her over but told us that she was already dead. We still called for the ambulance and she was taken to the hospital. Her grandmother and I went with her, but there was nothing that anyone could do. Dr. Williams went with us, and I heard some talk about the death certificate, which he wouldn't sign. Degar arrived later and made some arrangements with an undertaker who came and picked up the body. Degar told me that he was going to send the body to South Carolina to be buried with his mother, but I didn't go with them."

"What happened after that?"

"When he came back, he told me that he had burial insurance on Tess that took care of the expense."

"Did he tell you about any other insurance?"

"Yes, a few days later he received a check for $500 from the insurance company, and told me that we could get married."

"What happened then?"

"Things went along pretty well, but a few days later while he was at work I got to looking around where he kept a few things and there was a life insurance policy with my name on it payable to Degar as beneficiary."

"What did you do then?"

"I got to thinking about it. He had told me that he collected some insurance on his first wife, so I decided it was time for me to go to high ground. I gave the neighbor my address and took the train back to Cincinnati."

"Did you hear from him after that?"

"Yes, he wrote and asked me to return but I refused."

"No further questions."

Joshua Clayton began the cross-examination. "You lived in the house with the defendant, but you weren't married?"

"Yes, sir."

"Did you ever see him give any of the pills you spoke of to Tess Loghin?"

"No sir, he just left them on the table and told her to take them if she needed them."

"Did the bottle have any markings on it?"

"Yes, Bicarbonate of Soda."

"Did you actually see her take them?"

"No."

"And you never saw him give any of them to her?"

"No."

"No further questions."

The second day of the trial ended and court was adjourned. The defendant was taken back to the jail cell, and there followed the usual banter between the lawyers and the judge in his chambers. The judge chuckled, saying that the statement "arsenic and old lace" might be replaced with "strychnine and Trojans" after this case was finished.

"Clayton will be sorry he pushed Jackson on how he remembered Loghin. That's an example of a lawyer asking a question on cross-examination without anticipating the answer. He may have nailed his client," said Odom as he walked back to his office.

Chapter Twenty-seven

The first thing next morning, Odom placed Dr. Clarence Best on the stand.

"Did you ever have occasion to attend Tess Loghin?"

"Not as a patient, but I did accompany the undertaker and the sheriff to South Carolina where her body was exhumed. It was taken to the local hospital there."

"Did you perform an autopsy of her body?"

"Yes, I removed the liver, the kidneys, and the brain; I placed them in a sealed container and personally transported them to the Duke University Medical School toxicology department in Durham, North Carolina."

"Were they marked for identification?"

"Yes. We guard against identification mix-ups."

"What was done with them at Duke?"

"They were turned over to the toxicology department, under the direction of Dr. Jules Tayloe, for a chemical analysis."

"In connection with this case did you attend the exhumation of another body?" Clayton tried to object but he was overruled.

"Yes, sir, about a week later the sheriff and an under-taker exhumed the body identified as Ginny Loghin, who had died in July. Her hands were clenched, and she was taken to the mortuary. I removed the same organs I removed from the body of Tess Loghin. They were carefully identified and in turn taken to Duke for chemical analysis."

"Was anything else unusual found in the body?"

"Yes, there was a fetus, and based on its size I estimated it was in the third to fourth month of development."

"Did Dr. Jules Tayloe do the analysis on these organs also?"

"Yes."

"Do you know the results of the analysis?"

"Objection."

"Sustained."

"Did you personally examine the organs for chemicals?" Gardener asked on cross-examination.

"No."

"So, as far as you could tell they appeared to be normal in each case?"

"Yes."

"And you did not remove the heart of either of these bodies for examination?"

"No."

"Did you know that Ginny Loghin's death certificate indicated 'heart attack' as the cause of death?"

"Not at the time."

"Did you examine her heart?"

"No."

"No further questions."

Odom called Dr. Jules Tayloe next, and after giving his medical credentials and history he was qualified as an expert by the judge over Clayton's objection.

"Doctor, will you describe the circumstances regarding the organs delivered to you by Dr. Best?"

"Yes, they were delivered to me in a sealed container and upon opening it I found the brain, kidneys, and liver, apparently of a young person, marked as those of a Tess Loghin. I dissected them further and took samples of each for chemical analysis. I recovered about 34.04 milligrams, about half a grain, of strychnine from the brain and liver alone."

"Is there such a thing as a medical or therapeutic dose of strychnine?"

"Yes, that would be about two milligrams or less, so I found that she had absorbed about seventeen times what would be a normal dose."

"Is there a maximum amount of the poison which can be recovered by analysis of the organs?"

"The maximum amount that could be recovered would depend on how much was present. It's hard to say how much we can get out. We can't get more than is there."

"State what the percentage of recovery would be?"

"In my opinion this would vary between 10 and 25 percent of the amount that was there."

Clayton objected and made a motion to strike. He was overruled.

"Based on your findings of the amount of strychnine in her viscera, do you have an opinion satisfactory to yourself as to the cause of death?"

"Yes."

"What is it?"

Clayton and Gardener both objected and a conference was called at the judge's bench. After the discussion the objection was overruled and exception taken.

"That she died of strychnine poisoning."

"Was another set of organs given to you for examination at a later date?"

"Yes, the same set of organs, identified in the same manner as Tess Loghin's were delivered to me about a week later."

"What did the analysis show?"

"All of the tests showed characteristics of strychnine poisoning. Approximately twenty-two milligrams of strychnine were recovered from the liver and kidneys. In my opinion that's sufficient amount to cause death."

Clayton objected again and made another motion to strike the answer. The judge called the lawyers to his chambers for a conference. After they returned the judge made the following ruling, to which objection and exception was made:

"Although the defendant is not on trial for the murder of Ginny Loghin, evidence of another crime may be admitted when it tends to establish a common scheme or plan embracing the commission of a series of crimes so related to each other that proof of one tends to prove the other and show the defendant's guilt of the crime charged."

Clayton began his cross-examination. "Doctor, you never treated Tess Loghin, did you?"

"No."

"You know nothing about her general health before her death, do you?"

"No."

"Did you examine her heart?"

"No, I was only obtaining chemical analysis for poisons, and ordinarily poisonous substances will not appear in the heart tissue, so it wasn't examined."

"So as far as you know she could have died of a heart attack?"

"That's a possibility, but the amount of strychnine I found was enough to cause death."

"You didn't examine any part of her stomach or colon?"

"No."

"So if there was a problem in some other part of her body that could have caused or contributed to her death, you didn't find it?"

"Yes, that's true."

"But you only examined the organs that were brought to you?"

"Yes."

"You never treated Ginny Loghin either, did you?"

"No."

"Did you examine her heart at Duke?"

"No, I only examined the organs that were brought to me."

"Did you know that her death certificate attributed her death to 'heart attack'?"

"No."

"And you didn't treat her?"

"No."

"So heart attack could have been the cause of death?"

"Yes, but there was enough strychnine found in her organs to kill her."

"Isn't it true, doctor, that when rigor mortis sets in that there is usually a contraction of muscles which causes a clenching of the hands and an extension of the limbs and feet?"

"Yes, I've seen that many times."

"No further questions."

Odom placed Dr. Evan Jones on the stand and he was qualified as an expert witness. "Did you ever treat Tess Loghin?

"I didn't treat her, but on Thanksgiving Day last year Degar Loghin came to my house and asked me to come out and see his girl. She was sick in the car. We carried her into the house, where she continued to have violent convulsions and pain in her stomach. Mr. Loghin told me that the only medicine she had taken was B.C. Powder. I tried the best I could to find out what the problem was, and in the midst of her convulsions she would scream and ask me to do something for her, saying she was going to die. I sent her to the hospital and Dr. Champion attended her. I'm familiar with strychnine poisoning and its symptoms are marked by periodic convulsions and contraction of the hands and arms."

"Do you have an opinion as to what caused her condition?"

"Yes, it was strongly suggestive of strychnine poisoning."

Clayton renewed his cross-examination. "You never treated her?"

"No."

"Her problems in the stomach area could have been caused by overeating on Thanksgiving dinner?"

"That's true."

"Were you called to see her at the hospital on Thanksgiving day, or at the time of her death on December first?"

"No."

"So the only time you saw her was the few minutes at your house?"

"Yes."

"Isn't it true, doctor, that strychnine can be used as a tonic for therapeutic purposes?"

"Although I've never used it, I've read about a mixture of quinine, molasses, and strychnine as a tonic—some call it QMS—but I don't know its effect, and I believe it's an old home remedy."

Court was adjourned for the day and Emma accompanied Eliza Harper, Will Jackson, and the Ohio deputy to the train station and saw them off. The judge, Sheriff Dawkins, Dennis Coleman, Odom, Clayton, and Gardener went to an oyster roast place on the sound and feasted on boiled shrimp, fresh-roasted oysters, and johnny cake. For the time being they seemed to forget their adversarial differences, and exhibited a level of professionalism that was expected at the time. They enjoyed the shellfish along with a little bourbon. Good fellowship among the members of the bar and with the judges was usual and prominent in those days.

Chapter Twenty-eight

The next morning, Odom, Dennis, and Sheriff Dawkins met early.

"Well, we've finally reached the point where we have to put Dr. Champion and Dr. Williams on the stand," Odom said. "Williams isn't a problem. He didn't sign the death certificate because he didn't know the cause of death. Champion, however, apparently signed the certificate and listed 'idiopathic convulsions' as the cause. He was under pressure from the family to get it signed so that Tess' body could be shipped to South Carolina for burial. I'm afraid that this may cause confusion in the jurors' minds and lead to doubt, but we'll have to continue and go forward."

When court opened Dr. Champion was called as the first witness. He was introduced and qualified as an expert over Clayton's objection.

"Did you ever treat Tess Loghin?" Odom asked.

"Yes, last Thanksgiving I was on duty at the hospital and I received a call from Dr. Evan Jones. He told me that he was sending a patient to the hospital. As a result of that call I attended a young girl identified as Tess Loghin."

"What was her condition?"

"She was in violent pain, mostly in the stomach and lower body area, and she was having convulsions. She was crying for attention. After talking with Degar Loghin and the lady who was with him, I learned that Tess had eaten a fairly large Thanksgiving dinner, so I ordered that her stomach be pumped out and gave her medicines designed to settle any condition that might exist. I suspected that she might have contracted some kind of meningitis and ordered a spinal tap. I also thought that it might be some kind of epilepsy, but as a result of my conversation with her father I found no history of this. She seemed to be better, so I prescribed a sedative and kept her in the hospital that night."

"What was the result of your treatment?"

"Well, I saw her chart the next morning, and it indicated that after the sedatives were administered she had slept fairly well. I saw the patient that morning. She was perfectly conscious at the time, and she seemed to be a little depressed and drowsy from the excitement and sedative she received during the night. Her only complaint was of a headache and muscular soreness."

"When was she discharged from the hospital?"

"Later that morning."

"Doctor, let's assume that the jury should find from the evidence and beyond a reasonable doubt the following information: On Thanksgiving Day, the twenty-sixth of November, 1936, Tess Loghin, in violent convulsions, was carried to the hospital and given the treatment you spoke of. She was discharged on Friday. On Tuesday morning, the first of December, she was taken with

185

violent convulsions and died before the doctor arrived. Her body was rigid; her hands were clenched so tightly that the undertaker had to straighten out her fingers; she was buried in South Carolina on the third of December. Her body was exhumed December tenth; the kidneys, liver, and brain were taken to Dr. Jules Tayloe, a toxicologist at Duke University. A chemical analysis was made, and 34.04 milligrams of strychnine were found in her body. Have you an opinion satisfactory to yourself as to the cause of her death?"

"Yes, sir."

"What is it?"

"Strychnine poisoning."

Clayton objected and was overruled. He began his cross-examination and handed Dr. Champion a piece of paper. "Is this your signature on Tess Loghin's death certificate?"

"Yes, sir."

"When did you sign it?"

"A day after her death, at the request of the funeral director."

"What did you describe as the cause of death?"

"Idiopathic convulsions."

"Just what does that mean, Doctor?"

"It can mean a lot of things, or nothing. It's a medical term; let's say it's a term in the form of a question mark. Idiopathic comes from two Greek words, meaning diseases."

"Then you don't really know what caused the girl's death?"

"Frankly, no. I knew that she suffered convulsions before death, and that such convulsions could have been induced by several diseases."

"Did you order an analysis on the contents of her stomach?"

"Yes, but because it was Thanksgiving the Pathology department was closed, and when I checked on it after her death I found that the contents had been disposed of."

"You didn't examine her heart?"

"No. Even though she was quite sick when I saw her on Thanksgiving, her heart, except for beating at a slightly accelerated rate, seemed normal."

Odom came forward and began his redirect examination.

"Could the convulsions have been caused by strychnine poisoning?"

"Yes. Based on Dr. Tayloe's findings I am of the opinion that it was the cause of her distress on Thanksgiving, and the cause of her death."

Odom called Dr. Victor Williams to the stand and he gave his opinion that the cause of death was strychnine poisoning. Bill Gardener did the cross-examination. "Doctor, you saw the patient at the time of death?"

"I saw her after I arrived at the house, but she had already died and there was nothing I could do for her."

"Were you asked to sign the death certificate?"

"Yes."

"Why didn't you sign it?"

"Well, I didn't treat her and I didn't know her history. From the condition of her hands and feet, I couldn't determine the cause of death."

"So you don't know the cause of death?"

"I didn't at that time, but based on the later findings I have an opinion now."

Odom called two other doctors to the stand, who gave their

opinions that Tess' death was caused by strychnine poisoning. They both admitted that they had never treated Tess Loghin on Clayton's cross-examination. Odom called Dr. William Manchester.

"I'm the Surgeon General of the railroad and live in Wilmington," Manchester said when asked to identify himself for the jury.

"Did you ever have occasion to treat Tess or Ginny Loghin?"

"No."

"Do the records of the railroad dispensary indicate that Degar Loghin ever received any prescriptions for either of these persons?"

"No."

"Did the dispensary ever keep strychnine in stock?"

"Not to my knowledge."

"Did you ever to your memory have any dealings with Degar Loghin?"

"No."

On cross-examination Manchester explained that it was possible that Loghin could have purchased over-the-counter, nonprescription drugs at the dispensary. The railroad kept no record of those kinds of purchases.

Jason Smallbones, local agent for the Metropolitan life insurance company, was the next witness Odom called. "Were you familiar with Degar Loghin?"

"Yes, he purchased life insurance from me."

"What kind of insurance?"

"We call it debit insurance, because the account is debited weekly and small payments are collected each week to keep it in force."

"Did he purchase such a policy on his daughter, Tess Loghin?"

"Yes, he purchased two policies. One on April first, 1935, in the principal amount of $500, and another March sixteenth, 1936, in the amount of $500."

"Were the premiums paid on these policies?"

"Yes. He generally paid the premiums in their exact amount each week, but on November twenty-fifth, he paid the premiums through the week of December fourteenth."

"Was this different from his previous payments?

"Yes. It was two weeks in advance of any other payments he had made on other policies."

"After Tess died did he collect the policies?"

"Yes. On the sixth of December he came to the office with a death certificate, applied for payment, and was paid shortly thereafter."

"Are you familiar with any other insurance carried by Degar Loghin?"

"Yes. Back in July he got me to help him with a claim he had with an insurance company when Ginny Loghin died. The policy was with a Virginia company dated in 1922, and he filed a claim with them and was paid $750 on the policy. It had been purchased shortly after he married her in 1922."

"And these are the only policies you know about?"

"Yes sir."

On cross-examination Smallbones testified that it was regular and usual for a father to purchase life insurance on his wife and child, and that he sold such policies all the time.

Odom recalled Bill Woolvin, the undertaker, to the stand. "Mr. Woolvin, earlier you testified that there was a small burial policy on Tess Loghin."

189

"Yes, we sell these policies to help with death expenses."

"Tell us about this policy."

"It was taken out with our mutual burial association, in the amount of $100 on October twenty-eighth, 1936. The total premium was paid at that time. Since we'd handled the burial, the policy was collected and the proceeds applied against our bill."

"Isn't it normal for a man to purchase life insurance and burial insurance on his close relatives?" Clayton asked on cross-examination.

"Yes, I sell them all the time."

When Smallbones was dismissed Odom placed witnesses on the stand who, over the objection of the defendant's legal team, testified that Loghin had obtained and collected insurance on the death of his first wife in 1922 and that Grace Mann had died under similar circumstances.

Odom finally rested his case and Joshua Clayton made a motion to dismiss based mostly on the fact that there was no direct evidence that Degar Loghin had administered the strychnine to Tess, and that the death certificates showed other causes of death. The motion was dismissed, and the defendant's attorneys were directed to proceed with their evidence.

Chapter Twenty-nine

All through the trial, Jake tried to keep up with it by reading the voluminous newspaper reports each morning, and his classmates at school discussed it every day. They couldn't understand how a father could kill his daughter. Each morning and afternoon as he rode the trolley down the street by the courthouse, he could see the onlookers vying for a seat in the courtroom. He wished he could skip school and look too, but he had spent his day in court and had proudly shared his experience with his friends.

Odom, Dennis, and Sheriff Dawkins met in Odom's office the night after they had rested their case. They were all relieved and excited about the first part of the trial being over. Odom reviewed the evidence they had put in, and they couldn't think of any omissions that could cause a problem on appeal.

"The weakest part of our case is that there is no direct evidence of his administering the drug to either Tess or Ginny," said Odom. "I believe that there's enough circumstantial evidence to prove his deed beyond a reasonable doubt, but when Clayton argues that this is a thin thread to hang a guy's life on, some of the jurors are bound to have some doubt."

"We know what Loghin's going to say on the stand. If they put him on, he'll deny it completely. That's what he did when we first interviewed him. All during the trial he's sat there like a wooden Indian, showed no emotion, and very seldom conferred with his counsel," Dennis said.

"I doubt that I can break him down on cross-examination, but I'll give it a try. Maybe we'll get lucky. After he testifies I understand they'll try to put on some evidence of good character, and I doubt that we'll have to put on any rebuttal evidence, so the trial will probably end in a couple of days."

Across town in Joshua Clayton's office, he and Gardener were planning Degar Loghin's examination.

"Of course, we could just not put him on the stand, but he insists that he wants to testify, and in the face of that we would be remiss as lawyers not to let him," Gardener said. "He's always held up pretty well in his denials, but you can expect Odom to really try to blast him. If Degar gets mad and confused he may hurt himself worse than Odom's evidence has already hurt him."

"I'll try to show that he's a normal, hard-working family man struggling to support a wife and child, and that he had valid reasons for purchasing the strychnine. But the circumstances have piled up on him and he may not be able to save himself. It's ultimately up to him to convince the jury of his innocence. I can only help him along," Clayton added. Both groups were at it until late that night, but they were all promptly present in court when it was called to order the next morning.

The judge announced that the proceedings were with the

defendant and directed the defense to call its first witness.

With that Clayton called Degar Loghin, and in his gaunt and stoic manner, dressed in coat and tie provided by his attorneys, he stood up. He had been sitting quietly in his chair, and the whistling and thumping of the steam radiators in the courtroom had reminded him of his good days amidst the jets of steam in the roundhouse. He wondered why a deputy had brought a small boy in a scout uniform by his cell about a week ago who had stared through the bars at him. He had also mused over what the outcome of the trial would be, and what it might be like to be in prison and face a certain death and the hereafter. His thought was that his lot before, although not too good, was better then than now. He had prayed to God for vindication. When Degar was sworn in Clayton began.

"What's your name?"

"Degar Loghin."

"How old are you, and where do you work?"

"Thirty-nine, and I work at the railroad in the Maintenance department at the roundhouse. I've worked there over fifteen years, starting from when I was discharged from service in the war. I'm assistant foreman in the shops, and have a crew of about eight men who work with me to repair and maintain the locomotives."

"Were you ever married?"

"Yes, I married Tess' mother shortly before I went overseas during the war, and Tess was born in 1921. Grace had female troubles and died in 1922. After she died, I married Ginny, and she and I took Tess back to live with us. She had been living with the Manns, Grace's mother and father. Ginny died last July of heart trouble, and I'm not presently married."

"How did you come to Wilmington?"

"Well, I was raised in the country in South Carolina and worked on a farm with livestock and hogs. When I was about fifteen, there wasn't much to that so I began working with a lumber company that had a steam-driven sawmill. I learned right much about steam engines at the lumber company. When I was about nineteen I heard that the railroad had a shop to service its engines, so I came up and applied for a job and got one in the roundhouse. I worked there until I was drafted for service in the war, and I went overseas for about six months. After I came home the job was given back to me."

"Tell us about Tess."

"She was my only daughter, and I loved her very much since I had raised her from the time that her mother died. She went to school and had done fairly well in her studies, and I hoped that she could finish school and become a nurse. She had some digestive problems, and on Thanksgiving we all ate a large dinner and went for a ride. She became very sick and was having some kind of convulsions, so I took her to Dr. Evan Joneses house. He couldn't help her and sent her to the hospital where Dr. Champion treated her. She was well enough to be released the next day and she came home. She seemed fine after that, and was fine when I went to work early on December first. All I gave her was bicarbonate of soda tablets, which I got from the railroad dispensary. On the day she died Ginny called me at the shop and told me that she was having another spell of sickness. When the doctor was called and got there she was already dead; he couldn't do anything for her. They took her to the hospital and I met them there. We were all very upset. I looked at Tess lying on the table and broke down, but it was too late. Later I took her to South Carolina to be buried where my mother is buried."

"Did you ever purchase any strychnine?"

"Yes. I couldn't get it in Wilmington. I'd been told you could use it to treat dogs for worms, and from my experience on the farm, I knew that it could be used for hogs. I had an old dog who was weak and puny from worms and old age. While I was in Cincinnati I asked a druggist about it and bought some."

"Did you give it to the dog?"

"Yes, and unfortunately the dog died, but I don't think that killed her. She was pretty old and had about had it anyway."

"Did you have any other reason to purchase it?"

"Yes, times were very hard, and keeping food on the table with my little salary was getting harder. When I was a boy I had some experience in raising hogs, and I was planning to purchase a few and keep them in my back yard. I bought enough strychnine to have some to worm and treat the hogs when I got them."

"What did you do with it?"

"Well, because of hard times and no money, I never got around to getting the hogs, so the rest of the stuff was thrown away."

"Did you ever give any of it to Ginny Loghin?"

"No, I didn't."

"Did you ever give any to Tess Loghin?"

"No, I didn't."

"Did you leave it around where either of them could have taken it?"

"No, I threw it away in the trash. As God is my witness, I did not poison Ginny Loghin or Tess Loghin; they were my wife and daughter, and I loved them and took care of them."

"No further questions."

Odom was a little surprised at Degar's demeanor during his testimony; he was straightforward and to the point. His expression, although it didn't change much, was sincere, and his words were worthy of belief. Odom asked for a recess before he began his cross-examination.

When court was back in session Odom began. "You did purchase the strychnine in Cincinnati?"

"Yes, I told you that."

"And your wife Ginny died about a month after your return?"

"Yes."

"And you kept it around the house?"

"No, what I didn't use on Sis I kept in my locker at the shop until I could get the hogs."

"When did you get rid of it?"

"I don't remember exactly, but in October the price of hogs was so high that I gave up my plan and threw the rest in the trash at the railroad."

"You don't deny that you purchased insurance on Ginny Loghin, Tess Loghin, and Eliza Harper, do you?"

"No. Times were bad, and I wanted to be protected in case they died."

"But why would you get it on Eliza?"

"I expected to marry her."

"Isn't it true that you planned to murder Ginny when you bought the strychnine in May?"

"No, I loved her."

"And isn't it true that you had such an easy time killing Ginny that you killed Tess within five months thereafter?"

"No, she was my only child and I loved her."

"But you planned to kill both of them in order to collect the life insurance?"

"No, I did not."

"And you paid the premium on Tess' policy two weeks in advance so you would be sure that it was still in effect when the poison you gave her killed her?"

"No, I had a little extra money from overtime work, so I went ahead and paid it so that there would be more money around for Christmas. I loved Tess as my only daughter."

"Well, if you didn't give them the strychnine, how did they get it?"

"I don't know, but I do know that I certainly didn't give it to them."

"But before they died, they had been in good health?"

"Well Ginny was going to have a baby, and was having sickness like ladies usually do. Tess always had indigestion problems like she had on Thanksgiving. That's why I kept the bicarbonate of soda around."

"But when you gave them the strychnine it wasn't to help this?"

"I didn't give them the strychnine. I don't know how they got it, if they did."

"So you deny that you gave them the strychnine even though you purchased it?"

"I've told you that, and it's true. I didn't give it to them."

"But the truth is that you killed them both in order to collect life insurance on them and to marry Eliza Harper."

"That is not true. As God is my witness I never killed anybody."

"No further questions."

On redirect Degar again denied that he killed anyone and repeated that the purchase of insurance was what any father and husband would do with his wife and daughter.

Joshua Clayton then put on Jere Swain and Bob Callus who testified that they had known Degar Loghin for over ten years, and that he had an excellent character and reputation in the community.

Odom offered no rebuttal evidence, and announced to the court that the State would waive the opening argument and allow the defense to open so that he could have the closing argument. The court was adjourned with the announcement that the defense would begin arguments first thing in the morning. With this the lawyers left the courthouse filled with relief, but considering deep in their minds the seriousness of the next day, which would control Degar Loghin's fate.

Degar slept restlessly in his cell that night, but he was relieved that he had told his story and denied his guilt before the court and God.

Chapter Thirty

The day of closing arguments was a cold February day, and the hiss of the steam radiators in the courtroom augmented the murmurings of the observers as Judge Clawson opened court and directed the defense to proceed with its argument.

Then and all through the argument, Degar seemed to listen with attention, although the noise of the steam radiators reminded him of his workplace and made him wish that he was back in the roundhouse. His expression never changed during the arguments, but he continually faced the jury and nodded several times as Clayton spoke.

Joshua Clayton had argued many first-degree murder cases before and was a grizzled veteran who, although he defended each client with passion and skill, had great faith in the jury system and had never shown a bit of sympathy to the client when the death sentence was announced. He opened his statement with the usual reminder that the defendant sat there clothed with a "cloak of innocence," following this with an in-depth argument.

"You twelve gentlemen of the jury are here to judge the life or death of this man who is a hard working citizen of this city, who has served his country in time of war, and who has struggled for many years amid the grease, dirt, and steam at the railroad to provide a home for his wife and food and education for his daughter. He now stands accused of killing his daughter, and the solicitor has insidiously tried to inject into this trial incompetent evidence regarding his wife's death. You are charged with the solemn burden of finding beyond a reasonable doubt whether he is guilty or not guilty, and this is a sacred and responsible duty. If you find him guilty, he will lose his most valuable possession—his very life. This duty should be approached prayerfully and with deep thought, for, I say to you today, that there are so many doubts about the evidence placed before you that you can only bring a verdict of innocence.

"First, there is no direct evidence whatsoever that Degar Loghin administered to, or provided for, anything other than B. C. Powders to Tess Loghin, and there was no evidence of any other ingredient ever found in his house or where he worked. He purchased the strychnine for use in treating his old hound dog, which he did, but there is no evidence that the dog died of poisoning. It was old, and we all know that dogs in this area frequently die of heartworms.

"Likewise, there is no direct evidence that he had any disagreements with his daughter, or that any of his actions were life threatening. In fact, he has sworn on the stand here that he loved his daughter, and the evidence shows that he provided her with a home and worked hard so that she could attend school.

"The solicitor has tried to imply that the small amounts of

200

insurance he collected are a motive for murder, but each of you knows that it is reasonable and proper for a man to provide life insurance on his relatives in order to assure that they receive a decent burial. In each case here you will see that he respectfully, and with love, provided for their proper burial. If he really did kill them, wouldn't he have tried to hide the bodies? But such was not the case. He always contacted doctors, saw that they entered the hospital, and had an undertaker provide them with a sufficient and proper burial.

"After his wife died, he even brought in a housekeeper so that his daughter's burden around the house would be lessened. Is this an action that implies that he killed her? No, it implies that he wanted to continue to provide comfort to her.

"The State has placed much emphasis on the condition of Tess' limbs, hands, and feet after her death, but there is evidence from the undertaker and from a doctor that this can be caused by rigor mortis. This is common knowledge, and it raises a strong doubt as to the cause of death.

"In addition, the bodies were embalmed, and the powerful embalming fluids certainly permeated all the organs of the body, confusing their analysis. No explanation was made as to how this would have affected the organs. I say that there was no way to determine the cause of death from an examination of the organs after the body had been embalmed.

"Likewise there is no doubt that the death could have been caused by a heart attack, and no attempt was made to examine the condition of the heart after death.

"You will note that the solicitor waived his opening argument, and will close with a summation which will be delivered to you with intense passion, but please remember that I will not have a chance to rebut what he says, and carefully consider the doubts which I have tried to lay before you.

"So, I say to you that the evidence itself discloses many doubts in this case, and the evidence lacks sufficient proof to support a finding that this innocent defendant killed Tess Loghin or anyone else. You should bring in a verdict that will release Degar Loghin and let him return to his job and continue his life.

"I thank each of you for your attendance in accordance with your civic duty, and pray that each of you will consider my arguments and render a verdict of not guilty. You will then be able to return to your families knowing that you have served the State well and live always with a clear conscience." He sat down and nodded to the defendant, who showed no response and maintained his solemn countenance.

Odom smiled, rubbed his hands together, and discharged his last bite of Indian Chew into the spittoon near the prosecutor's table. He arose, gathered his coat around him, leisurely walked toward the jury box, and faced the jury. "I too am here with the solemn duty delegated to me by the State of North Carolina to convince you of the guilt of this defendant, Degar Loghin, and to protect the State from any additional murders.

"In the little house on Beach Road about a year ago there were three toothbrushes hanging in the bathroom side by side; now there is only one. Three people were alive and well in that house. One, Tess Loghin, was a young girl in the bloom of life attending school and enjoying her friends. One, Ginny Loghin, was a housewife, taking care of the man she married and loved, and preparing to give him the greatest gift of all, a new child. But what was Degar Loghin doing? He was going to Ohio, where he met a young lady, purchased a deadly poison, and planned a method to end the lives of his wife and child. He returned in June and tested the poison on his poor dog; he found it successful, and in July his wife Ginny Loghin died. Sufficient amounts of strychnine were found in her body to lead the doctors to believe that it killed her. In November following, on our blessed holiday of Thanksgiving, he administered strychnine to Tess Loghin hoping to hide its effect by the ruse of too much Thanksgiving dinner. He failed that time, but it didn't stop him. Four days later Tess was stricken with the same symptoms and died in excruciating pain even before the doctor could arrive to help her. Poor Ginny. Poor Tess.

"He had planned it carefully. He already had insurance on Ginny, but it was a little different with Tess. He didn't purchase the insurance on her until March and April 1936, and even paid the premium two weeks in advance in November to make sure that the deadly potion would have time to work. He even hedged his bet a little more by buying a burial insurance policy on Tess.

"And what about Eliza Harper, who I believe is completely innocent in the matter? She appeared in town within a month of Ginny's death to 'housekeep' for Degar and make Tess' burden lighter. But there is no doubt in my mind that the trip to Ohio and the presence of a new young body was an incentive to destroy another body.

"In order to have first-degree murder it must be premeditated and carried out with malice aforethought. What could be more premeditated than purchasing a poisonous substance, bringing it into your home, and making it available to the persons whom you wish to dispose of? The malice aforethought becomes so obvious from this that I will not dwell on it anymore. Well, what was the motive? There are two motives readily apparent. The insurance money, although small, was certainly an incentive and a moving reason for Degar Loghin to dispose of his wife and daughter. He had struggled in the grease and steam of the railroad to maintain his family, but he never had $1,000 at one time. He did it for the money.

"Also the lure of a younger wife motivated him. But Eliza Harper was smart. Even with a promise of marriage in the offing, the first time she saw her name on an insurance policy she left for Ohio—went back to high ground! If I had seen my name on an insurance policy in that house, the moon would not have been high enough ground for me! To make things worse, he left poor Eliza home with Tess after he had provided in some way for administering the fatal dose. It was Eliza who tried to comfort her in her dying agony, and it was Tess' grandmother who arrived at the moment of death, who had the foresight to disclose this murderer to the sheriff. Mrs. Mann even implies that Degar killed *her* daughter years ago. It was this distant memory that sparked the investigation, clearly shows murder in the first degree, and brings Degar Loghin before this court so that justice can be administered.

"Degar Loghin knew that Tess died of poisoning. If he didn't know, why would he be in such a hurry to ship the body to South Carolina for burial? He was afraid of an autopsy. Likewise, his murder of Ginny was hidden by the cause of 'heart attack' on her death certificate. But the autopsy, and the examination of her body, clearly shows otherwise.

"The defense makes a point of the confusion in the causes

of death between the doctors involved; you must remember that a poison death is a rare and unusual thing, and that many doctors never see one in a lifetime of practice. Once the autopsy was performed, and the results obtained, none of the doctors had any doubt about the cause and have so testified in this courtroom.

"So the malice aforethought was there, the motive was there, the method was there, and Tess Loghin died after a fatal dose of poison was administered to her. The State has proved beyond a reasonable doubt that Degar Loghin is guilty of murder in the first degree, and you should so find!"

With that last blast, which could be heard through the closed windows by the curious standing in the street below, Odom thanked the jury for their attention and for fulfilling a public duty and returned to his chair.

The judge announced a recess, indicating that he wished to confer with the lawyers before charging the jury.

At the conference Judge Clawson advised the parties of the instructions he planned to give the jury with regard to circumstantial evidence, and his allowing the admittance of evidence regarding Ginny Loghin's death. Clayton again argued against any instruction that would indicate the guilt of his client with regard to Ginny's death and was again overruled. After this discussion court was reopened.

Judge Clawson instructed the jury of the meaning of murder in the first degree, reviewed the contentions of the State and the Defense, reminded them of their solemn duty, and sent them to the jury room for deliberation.

When the jury retired the lawyers milled around the court-room, smoking and chatting. Odom took a big bite from his

Indian Chew bar and addressed Dennis Coleman. "Well, I guess we did the best we could. I feel good about the jury and believe that they'll give it a fair deliberation. We certainly gave them all we've got, but if we lose, I'll set the trial for Ginny Loghin's death as soon as possible."

On the other hand, Bill Gardener and Joshua Clayton were not as relaxed. Although Joshua knew several members of the panel personally, their demeanor during argument was not to his liking. Degar was taken to his cell to await the verdict.

It took exactly three hours and ten minutes for the jury to return. Degar was brought back into the courtroom, and Judge Clawson asked the foreman if they had reached a verdict.

"We have, your honor."

"Hand it to the clerk."

The judge glanced at it and gave it back to the foreman. He directed the defendant to stand. Degar slowly stood up as did the entire courtroom, the solicitor, and defense attorneys.

The foreman cleared his throat and slowly read: "We find the defendant, Degar Loghin, guilty of murder in the first degree of Tess Loghin."

With the vivid announcement of these condemning words, the wooden-Indian expression on Degar's face didn't change, but he did sit down, drop his head, clasp his hands, and stare at his feet.

Clayton requested that the jury be polled, and when the judge asked each member if "guilty" was his verdict they all responded in the affirmative.

As there was no provision for a sentencing hearing, Judge William Clawson made the following pronouncement:

"Degar Loghin, you have been found guilty of murder in the

first degree of Tess Loghin by a jury of your peers; pursuant to the statutes made and provided by the State of North Carolina, I direct that you be transferred to the state prison in Raleigh, and on the last Friday in April next be executed until you are dead in the State's lethal gas chamber. And may God have mercy on your soul."

The trial was over, the bailiff returned Degar to his cell, and all left the courtroom in a somber mood.

There was neither relative nor friend there to console Degar in his loss.

Chapter Thirty-one

The next morning Odom spoke to Sheriff Dawkins. "Sheriff, of course, as we all know, there is an automatic appeal when there is a sentence of death, but thankfully that will be handled by the attorney general's office in Raleigh. I want to thank you for all your good work, especially by Dennis Coleman. Unless Degar gets a new trial we'll be through for a while."

In due time the appeal was filed in Raleigh. Arguments were held, with Clayton emphasizing the contended error made by the judge in allowing evidence concerning Ginny Loghin's death. The court sustained the judge's ruling on this. Shortly afterward, the Supreme Court of North Carolina affirmed the conviction.

The defendant was executed very soon thereafter. He was the first person to die in the newly-constructed lethal gas chamber. A few witnesses attended, including Joshua Clayton, who was with his client to the end, even after presenting a petition for leniency.

Loghin's only comment to the chaplain who attended him after he ate his last supper was, as always: "As God is my witness, I did not kill Tess Loghin!'

There was no family or friend to accompany the wooden, state-provided casket that came out of the back of the prison to be buried in a pauper's grave.

That day all the trains left on time.

Emma was particularly glad that the matter was over, for she could again have Dennis with her as they awaited the birth of their first child.

Jake had mixed feelings about the outcome; even though he felt that Tess' death was avenged, he had many doubts as to whether the quiet death in the gas chamber was sufficient punishment for the pain and suffering given Tess by her father.

Sarah and Caleb were of little comfort to him, so he took it up with his lifelong confidante Carrie, who was still faithfully serving his family.

"Carrie, I don't think that it's fair that he was executed. I think he should have been placed in prison forever, and each day reminded of his daughter and wife and how he deprived them of all life and future."

"Jake, don't you worry about him not being punished. He breathed that gas and went to sleep easily, but before he wake, dat devil man grabbed him and put the fire to him, and he gonna wish he had never seen no wife and chile, much less put de poison to them. Jake, you can bet his punishment will be 'ternal, while Tess, with the love of the Lawd, will be happy forever in that house in heaven dat de 'postle John said she and her mamma would find. But Jake, you know de Lawd has so much love and forgiveness in Him, He jus might someday bring that man up there and find a place for him, too."

Jake walked over to the woods, pondering the tangled events that had consumed his life for the last few months.

Later he enjoyed recalling the happy times he had spent with his youthful friends. He became a lifeguard at the beach as he had told Tess he wanted to become. He also became a lawyer and enjoyed hunting and fishing, which they had talked about many times. The sad parts of Tess' life slowly faded away and he always remembered her in a happy manner. His best memory of all was Carrie's all encompassing arms and her God-nurtured philosophy, which had helped him into manhood.

Author's Note

Although this book is written as a novel, it is based on a North Carolina case in 1936, reported at the Supreme Court in the Spring Term of 1937 in Volume 213 NC 79 as *State v. Smoak*. The victim in that case was a classmate of the author until she was killed during her third high school year.

The real hero in that case was Superior Court Judge John J. Burney, then District Attorney, who, with limited investigative sources brought together some twenty-five witnesses, including seven doctors, and prosecuted the case without assistant district attorneys to help him, resulting in the conviction. The trial is a leading case on the use of circumstantial evidence and expert witnesses in criminal cases, and has frequently been cited as authority on these points.

The author in later years appeared before Judge Burney in many cases, the most important of which was when the Judge swore him into the practice of law with the admonition: "Stay in your office and always promptly answer your phone calls." Instructions well heeded and kept.

I refrain from making editorial comment on how quickly the trial was held, the verdict returned, the appeal made, and the sentence carried out as compared to today.

Reports contained in the *Wilmington Morning Star* were reviewed and used as references. Additionally, an article in the August 1937 issue of *Front Page Detective,* published by Exposed Publishing Company was used as a reference.

Street Cars

Th

The Orton Hotel